City of Fear

RICHARD JAMES

First published in 2020 by Sharpe Books.

Contents

The following two short stories take place after the events of the third novel in the Bowman Of The Yard series, THE BODY IN THE TREES.

THE CAMDEN KIDNAPPINGS

AUGUST, 1892

The Regent's Canal had seen busier times. Constructed to provide a link between the Limehouse Basin in the east and the Grand Union Canal to the west, it had fallen victim to the railways. Its banks had once been worn by the hooves of a thousand horses charged with heaving the narrowboats through the water, straining at their harnesses as they struggled for purchase. Time was that the span of the canal would have been crowded with cargo; hay and straw bound for sale at Cumberland Market, fruit and vegetables for the East End. The boatmen would urge each other on with the most colourful language they could find, heedless of the children that led the horses along the bank. Craft of all lengths had once crowded at the locks, eager to resume their progress. Only at their final destination would the boatmen be paid and so every obstacle, every impediment to their journey, was greeted with a surly disdain. If the cargo was even half a day late, their pay would be docked.

The coming of the railways had only served to make life harder still. A delivery that would, by canal, have taken two days could now be made in a quarter of the time. As a consequence, the canal towpaths had become overgrown and ill-maintained. Those few horses that were left to haul the craft along the erstwhile arteries of the canal system had now no choice but to pick their way carefully through the treacherous knots of weeds and bracken that had quickly sprung up by the canal side, slowing progress even further.

The Regent's Canal wound its way lugubriously through King's Cross, Euston and Camden, swilling occasionally in deep basins where the occasional narrowboat would even now moor to unload its burden. More regularly, however, boats were abandoned and scuppered, either in the basins or far from the

1

canal network in wider rivers. Their owners, unable to continue with their work and unable to afford the salvage fees, had elected instead to simply drown their boats. Their skeletons tilted at alarming angles as they fell prey to the mud, their innards plundered by looters and chancers as if they were so much carrion. All in all, it was looking like the narrowboat's days were numbered. Skippers scrambled for such commissions as they could, lowering their prices almost every day to compete with the quicker, more efficient engines. The railway, particularly in the more rural areas just outside the capital, often passed alongside the canals or over its bridges, the trains whistling merrily as they sped past, rubbing salt into the wound.

These days, it took a special breed of man to skipper a narrowboat. One such man was Peregrine Evans. Evans had grown into his Christian name. In seeming imitation of the hawk for which he was named, a mane of jet black hair was greased back from a widow's peak, accentuating a prominent nose that seemed to lead the way before him. A pair of sharp eyes glinted with malevolent intent beneath the shelf of his brow. He seemed constantly to be in a state of agitation, his slender but barrel-chested frame leaning forward on the balls of his feet as if in anticipation of the kill, his long yellow talons hooked around the tiller. A hand-rolled cheroot hung damp from his mean lips as if it were nothing more than a recent kill, a small, scurrying mammal, perhaps, that he had snatched from the banks of the canal. He was dressed in a pair of too-short felt trousers that swung about his ankles and his only shirt, the sleeves rolled up to the elbows. It was worn open at the neck, where a tattered and greasy neckerchief hung limp and with a distinct lack of panache. A loose waistcoat with no buttons hung open around his waist.

As he rounded the bend into Hawley Lock, Peregrine Evans squawked to his companion on the bank to slow the horse. Jenny was a girl of eleven. Of average stature for her age, she was in every way unremarkable save for the fact that she had, unfortunately, inherited her father's nose. She walked barefoot along the bank, her frayed frock tied at the waist with a piece of string. Although she had known nothing beyond being a boatman's daughter and had no education to speak of, she knew enough to know it wasn't for her. She had, in her time, walked almost the entire length of the Grand Union Canal, and dreamed of a life in service in one of the many country houses she had seen on the horizon. The narrowboat had occasionally been met by grand carriages come to collect a delivery of ice or canvas for the use of Lord and Lady Such-and-such at their latest summer party. One of the less haughty drivers had once told Jenny how she might earn a penny a week as a maid of all work. The thought of it had made her heart race, until her father had put her straight in no uncertain terms.

'You're fit for nothing but leadin' an 'orse,' he had breathed, 'Don't be getting ideas above yer station.' With that, he had drawn upon his cheroot and turned his head to the wind as if to indicate he would admit no further discourse in the matter. Jenny had swallowed her tears and vowed to prove her father wrong. She liked nothing more than the thought of donning a pressed and starched uniform of a morning, no matter how thankless the work. She would even have a bed of her own, she was sure.

'Jenny!' She was drawn from her reverie by the harsh sound of her father's voice from the narrowboat. 'Unhitch him and get him to water!'

Evans' nag had the slow and steady gait of a horse well struck in years. Grey whiskers grew in profusion around his pink nose and dark, rheumy eyes. The boatman had won him in a bet during a particularly fortuitous - and drunken - game of whist. As the game had progressed, so Evans had become emboldened by drink. In need of a new horse since his other had given up the ghost, Evans had bet the entire contents of his narrowboat against a competitor's horse. Luckily, he had won. The horse was slow and steady and had weight enough to pull a fully laden narrowboat. Evans had never known him break into anything approaching a canter, even when let off the harness to graze. For this very reason, he had been given the ironic sobriquet, Stephenson's Rocket, or Rocket for short.

Jenny reached up to take the bit from Rocket's mouth and unhitch his harness. He gazed down at her with indifferent eyes and allowed himself to be led along the towpath to the water pump, his tail flicking lazily behind him.

Evans threw a rope to the lock-keeper and jumped onto the opposite bank. He hadn't seen this man before. With the fall in trade along the canal, so the post of the full time lock-keeper had been abolished. Now, each lock could be manned by any number of men in the Regent's Canal and City Docks Railway Company's employ. Between them, they would operate to a haphazard rota of sorts, manning any lock along the canal's length on any given day, sometimes only for the few hours that the lock was at its busiest. Evans sighed. The cottage that stood on the bank was once home to the lock-keeper and his family. Now, it stood empty and boarded against all visitors, its soft brick walls and wooden window frames left to crumble and rot in the elements. Taking up another cable at the boat's stern, the boatman helped to steady the craft and pull it into the lock. Casting his eyes beyond the lock's bottom gates, Evans could see where the level of the canal fell a good eight feet.

'That's a lot of timber,' the lock-keeper shouted, indicating the carefully stacked lengths of wood piled high in the narrowboat's hold. 'At least you'll have something to grab a hold of if you sink!'

The lock-keeper laughed at his own joke. Evans allowed a

smirk to turn the corners of his mouth, though whether as a display of mirth it was difficult to tell.

'Where you headin'?'

'West on the Grand Union,' Evans grumbled from between clenched teeth. He could not abide small talk. 'The timber's for a new station at Aylesbury.'

'That'll be another nail in the coffin for the Regent's then.' The lock-keeper shook his head sadly as he secured his rope to a mooring bollard.

'Reckon so.' Evans agreed.

As the lock-keeper straightened up to wipe the sweat from his brow with his kerchief, Evans cast his beady eyes back up the canal. Hawley Lock was the middle of a flight of three that served this bend in the canal. Kentish Town Lock lay a furlong behind him, the Hampstead Road Locks three quarters ahead. He had passed the previous without hindrance and could already see there would be no waiting at Hampstead Road. Beyond that, Evans knew, lay an easy nineteen mile stretch of canal to the west and the Grand Union Canal. He was looking forward to the more open vistas of the countryside. The Regent's Canal, particularly here at Camden, had little to recommend it. Evans and his craft had spent most of the morning in the shade of the tall buildings that rose like steep cliffs on either side. Workhouses, mills and wharves crowded right to the water's edge at some places, making Rocket's progress all the harder. Jenny was well practised at steering him gently through the narrower sections of the towpath, but even so, progress had slowed to a crawl. Often the rope had run slack between horse and boat, and Evans had had to shout to gee the creature on.

'Keep 'im at it, girl,' he had called to Jenny, 'I'll overtake you both at this rate!'

Though the traffic along the canal had been sparse, still the route had been filled with the noise of the city. Engines pounded rhythmically from behind the dark walls and steam belched from blackened chimneys into the summer sky, competing with the clouds as it rose in great puffy plumes. The sounds of hammers striking metal and saws cutting wood had rung out across the canal, echoing along its length in a cacophony of industry. Peregrine Evans longed for the more open reaches of the Grand Union, where only birdsong broke the still air.

For now, he blinked in the glare of the August sun on the water. Save for a child in a small homemade coracle, his was the only craft on the canal. Even five years previously, the picture would have been very different indeed. If Evans had been of an empathetic bent, he would undoubtedly have felt sorry for the lock-keeper. As it was, he was more concerned for himself. To maintain his narrowboat was costly and, with two mouths to feed and a horse to keep, he was feeling the pinch. With so much cargo moving about the country on the railways, he had noticed a decline in trade. Things were changing, of that there was no doubt, and Peregrine Evans did not care for change.

The narrowboat secured, Evans looked across to the opposite bank. The lock-keeper had his back to the balance beam at the top gate, and was waiting in expectation. Evans threw the soggy stump of his cheroot to the ground. Time was he would have stayed aboard and the lock-keeper's assistant would have helped. Now, he couldn't afford an assistant. With a nod to Evans as the boatman put his weight to the beam, the lock-keeper strained against the weight of water. Bracing his hobnailed boots on the ground, he walked gingerly backwards, his half of the gate closing slowly in the chamber beneath him.

'My father worked this canal all his life,' the lock-keeper breathed as he strained against the water. Evans nodded absently. 'Reckon we'll be closing it soon.'

Evans pushed against his own beam. Soon, like some huge,

aquatic beast held captive in the chamber, his narrowboat bobbed and strained against its moorings. At just shy of sixty feet long and seven wide, it was accommodated with room to spare. From the corner of his eye, Evans saw movement among the timber on the deck. Rats. He cursed to himself and made a promise to take a feral cat from the canal side just as soon as he got a chance.

'Where's yer timber from?' The lock-keeper was resting with his hands on his hips.

'France,' Evans deigned to respond. 'Come on the railway from Dover to King's Cross.'

The lock-keeper tutted. 'Can't even grow our own trees no more,' he muttered under his breath. He ran his fingers through a tangle of hair as he walked the length of the lock to the bottom gate. Moodily, he swung a handle into a ratchet and put his weight against it. As the lock-keeper turned the handle, Evans noticed a gentle movement on the surface of the water in the chamber. Little eddies swirled around the narrowboat's hull. Inch by inch, as the paddle was raised beneath the lock gates, so the waterline fell and Evans's boat with it. The boatman walked the length of the lock to ready himself on the bottom gate opposite the lock-keeper.

Glancing over the lock-keeper's heaving shoulders, Evans saw Rocket lapping from an old bucket that stood beneath the water pump. Jenny, it seemed, had left him to it.

'Good for nuthin' girl,' Evans hissed, 'Off explorin' when there's work to be done.' The young waif had been given her orders for the morning when they had left King's Cross Basin. 'Just as soon as we reach Camden,' Evans had instructed her over a meagre breakfast of oats, 'You must fix the horse's harness. It's rubbing on his hind quarters and I can't afford for him to go lame.' Jenny had nodded absently. It came as no surprise at all, then, to see that she had abandoned her charge at the water pump.

'It's no life for a young'un,' the lock-keeper pronounced, unbidden.

'How's that?' Evans took his cigarette papers and a pouch of tobacco from his trouser pockets.

'There's no future in the canals,' the lock-keeper panted, taking the handle from the ratchet. 'A few years ago they were petitioning to run a railway right along here.' He gestured along the banks. 'Reckon they might do it yet.' The lock-keeper gave a nod to the narrowboat in the chamber. 'You'd be better off learning how to drive an engine.'

'They'll still need their coal,' Evans retorted, 'And they'll still need boats to carry it.' The lock-keeper snorted at the irony. Evans grunted as he clamped a cheroot between his mean lips. 'It's a good enough life for me,' he rasped, striking a match against the balance beam, 'It'll be good enough for Jenny.'

At last, the level of the water in the chamber had fallen to that of the pound beyond. At a signal from the lock-keeper, Evans put his back to the balance beam and pushed. As he leaned against the beam, Evans gazed again across the water to his horse on the other side. There was still no sign of Jenny. Between them, Evans and the lock-keeper heaved open the bottom gates until the narrowboat's course was clear. The top of the wheelhouse now stood a good four feet below the level of the chamber's brick sides, and Evans loped towards the ladder set in the lock walls, untying the rope at the mooring.

'Jenny!' he called, half-absently, 'Get that horse hitched!' As he swung his leg over the top of the ladder, he cast a look back across the water. Rocket was tearing at a patch of weeds with his old teeth, clearly content to be left alone. Evans paused in his descent, his fingers gripping the rungs like claws.

'Where is that girl?' he seethed, 'We got to be on our way.'

The lock-keeper was concerned enough to look, too. Walking

towards the boatman's aged horse, he held out a hand to take it by the harness.

'No sign of her,' he said, uneasily.

Puffing his cheeks out in exasperation, Evans crossed the deck of his boat and heaved himself up a ladder on the opposite wall.

'She'll be the death of me,' he hissed from between clenched teeth. He walked with ever increasing haste to where the lock-keeper stood. Scanning the area with his beady eyes, Evans saw the lock-keeper's dilapidated cottage to his right and a dark alley before him. On one side rose the sheer walls of a saw mill, on the other, the windowless facade of a workhouse. Detritus littered the floor, collecting in drifts by dingy doorways and alcoves.

'Jenny!' the boatman called, a note of rising panic in his voice. Taking several steps into the alley before him, he cupped his hands to his mouth and called again. 'Jenny!' Despite the summer sun, Peregrine Evans felt a chill rising within him. Perhaps it was the cool of the shade between the two sheer buildings on either side that froze his blood. Or perhaps it was the fact that, as he and the lock-keeper began a cursory search of the immediate vicinity, Jenny Evans was nowhere to be found.

Detective Sergeant Anthony Graves had never felt so disheartened. It had fallen to him to clear Inspector Bowman's office of his effects and papers. Whether it was expected that he should ever return, the young sergeant did not know. Nor did he wish to guess. As the sun streamed in at the windows, Graves busied himself emptying drawers and shelves of files and folders. Placing each in turn into one of two large crates he had requisitioned from Scotland Yard's lost property department, he fought hard to resist an overwhelming feeling of loss. The affair at Larton had clearly cost Detective Inspector Bowman dear, but its effect upon Graves could not be underestimated. Never before had he seen a man in such despair, and never before had he felt so helpless in the face of events. Pausing to take stock, he let his clear blue eyes wander along the now empty shelves. He half expected to see the inspector himself leaning against them or sitting behind his desk at the window. Finally, his gaze fell upon Bowman's map of London. It spanned almost the entire length of the wall and showed in detail every street, alleyway and courtyard from Plumstead Marshes to Mortlake. In some areas even particular buildings were marked, so that it was possible to pinpoint with some accuracy the houses, tenements and landmarks that had featured so heavily in Bowman's recent investigations. Reaching up with a finger, Graves located the very building in which he stood, Scotland Yard, standing sentinel on the north bank of the Thames at Westminster. Just a hand's span away, he was able to find The Silver Cross on Whitehall, Smithfield Market, St. Saviour's Dock, the police house on Upper Grange Road and the Hackney Workhouse where Inspector Hicks had so disgraced himself. It all seemed so long ago now, part of a different life entirely. In truth, it had been only three weeks since Bowman had been removed from his duties. Graves flicked a stray blond curl from his forehead as he bent to the bureau beneath the map. Retrieving a key from his waistcoat pocket, he unlocked the flap and swung it open to reveal its contents. A decanter, little more than a third full, reflected the sunlight into a kaleidoscope of colours around the room. Gingerly, Graves transferred it to one of the crates on Bowman's desk, along with a glass and battered hip flask. His work done, the detective sergeant walked to the windows that gave out to the River Thames beyond. The Victoria Embankment seemed to glimmer in the summer heat and Graves had to squint against it to see. The river was busy with craft of all sizes. Small ferry boats flitted between the banks as fast as their oarsmen could row, a steamer chugged lazily beneath Westminster Bridge and there, in the distance, Graves could see the rigging of the sailing vessels waiting to berth at St. Katherine Docks. Nearer the bank, urchins dug for treasure, or indeed anything that could be sold for a penny, in the mud. They waded knee deep in the filth so that, as they emerged onto the bank, Graves could see the whole of their lower legs and feet were caked in an unctuous filth. The morning sun was glancing off the river to reflect on the buildings on the far bank. Graves felt like he was being treated to his own, private light show. As he turned back into the room, he shook his head to clear it. Bending to lift a crate of papers from the desk, he wondered what the day would bring. His answer came by way of a sudden commotion at the door. Lifting his gaze, Graves was greeted with the sight of a not inconsiderable bulk of a man filling the door frame.

'Ah, Graves,' boomed Detective Inspector Hicks with such volume that he might be heard across the River Thames, 'I see you're almost done.'

Graves noticed the portly inspector had a box of his own clasped between his huge, sweaty hands.

'I have taken all I can,' the sergeant replied, 'Although there are certain personal effects I feel we should leave for now.' He nodded towards the map on the wall.

'Oh, I shan't be needing that.' Hicks swayed into the room, dislodging great plumes of dust from the rug with his heavy boots. He slammed his box down upon the desk next to Graves' and arched his back to stretch it. 'I've got the whole of London housed up here,' he tapped at his forehead with a sausage of a finger, 'I have no call for maps.'

Graves stood for a moment, blinking in confusion. Slowly, he made sense of the scene. 'You're to take possession of Inspector

Bowman's office?' he breathed in disbelief.

Ignatius Hicks nodded, his hands planted on his hips. He looked around the room as a prospector might survey his newly acquired land. 'I am that,' he beamed. 'Waste not, want not.'

'But,' Graves stammered, incredulous, 'Inspector Bowman - '

'I don't think he'll be joining us any time soon, Graves,' Hicks took his pipe from a pocket and tapped it against an empty shelf. 'Do you?' Jamming the bit between his teeth in a gesture of defiance, Hicks reached into another pocket and threw a pouch of tobacco on the desk. It was, Graves felt, a signal of ownership.

The young sergeant breathed hard to restrain himself. 'Has it been approved?'

'By whom?' Hicks roared, his great beard jutting proudly before him. 'It is of no concern to anybody where I have my office.' Hicks strode to the window to take in the view. His view. 'But it is, without doubt, an improvement upon my previous room. The aspect alone will be most conducive to my work.' Swinging round upon his heels, Hicks threw himself into Bowman's chair. 'Yes,' he murmured to himself as he settled, 'Most conducive, indeed.' Reaching for his tobacco, he proceeded to feed a quantity into the bowl of his pipe with his fat fingers, his eyes flitting around the room. 'I should like that bureau moved closer to the door and those shelves will be perfect for my pipe collection.'

Before Graves could take the breath to object, there came a sharp knock at the door behind him. Turning, he saw Sergeant Matthews sporting a look of confusion at the sight before him.

'Sergeant Graves,' he began, breathlessly, his eyes flicking occasionally to the portly form behind Bowman's desk, 'You are to attend an address in Gloucester Crescent. I have the details of the case at my desk.'

Graves nodded in response, grateful for the diversion. 'I'll lug these crates to the stores and I'll be with you.'

'Gloucester Crescent, eh?' Hicks interjected from his desk as he lit the tobacco in his pipe. 'That's Chelsea way, I believe.' He tapped his forehead with a finger, meaningfully.

'Camden,' Matthews retorted from the doorway. 'Near the canal.'

Nonplussed, Hicks nodded slowly, as if Matthews had merely confirmed his assertion.

'Perhaps,' began Sergeant Graves as he retrieved a crate from the desk, 'We should leave that map where it is for now.'

'Where you goin'?' barked the driver from his perch.

Graves had been relieved to see a line of waiting hansom cabs on the Embankment, each awaiting a fare. Several of the drivers sat alert for passengers, while others had fallen asleep in the sun, their heads nodding forwards to rest awkwardly on their chests.

'Gloucester Crescent, Camden,' the sergeant replied, pulling his identification papers from a pocket.

Graves looked around him as he spoke, enjoying the spectacle of the activity about him. Impressive-looking men in impressive-looking attire made their way to the Palaces of Westminster, the height of their silk top hats seeming to denote their place in society. A gaggle of clergymen dodged the traffic as they crossed the road by Westminster Bridge, hitching their robes above their ankles as they skipped anxiously between the piles of horse dung and general detritus. At the sergeant's feet, two young children fought to catch a mangy dog that had escaped their clutches. Grabbing it by the scruff at last, they scuttled away at speed at Graves' mention of his occupation.

The cabbie gave a pretence of scrutinising Graves' papers then sat back in his seat, evidently satisfied that the sergeant was to be trusted.

Sergeant Graves jumped aboard and closed the folding wooden doors that would protect his legs and feet from the dust and dirt of the journey.

A flick of the driver's whip saw the horse spring into action. Soon, the pretty chestnut mare was at a trot, pulling the cab between the traffic with such a show of agility that Graves could not help but be impressed. The roads were at their busiest this time of day and, more than once, the cabbie had to retreat to the narrower side streets to avoid the congestion.

'What's the case?' leered the driver from his seat as they passed through Whitehall, 'A murder?'

Graves shook his blond curls in response. 'Not today,' he shouted back, cheerfully.

'Shame,' the driver called above the hubbub of the street, 'I love a grisly murder.'

The sergeant smiled. As the cab rattled over Seven Dials, he reflected on just how large a proportion of the populace felt the same. Certainly, as far as the newspapers and penny dreadfuls were concerned, murder was money. Many an edition of the Evening Standard had been sold on the promise of 'Another Grisly Murder - Details Within!'. He had seen it, too, during the course of his investigations. Periodically, he had found himself in some dark alley or other with only his fellow detectives for company, scratching at the ground for clues or rifling through a body for marks of foul play. Lifting his head, Graves was often surprised by a congregation of gawpers, each of them leering over another's shoulder for a better view. The human capacity for morbid titillation seemed insatiable, but Sergeant Graves found the impulse easy to forgive. In truth, he felt it himself. The thrill of a new case was something that had surprised him in the early days. It had felt an illicit pleasure, somehow, not to be spoken of. A guilty secret, even. Now, Graves recognised it as a strength. He had learned there was a pleasure to be had in the pursuit of a case and, particularly, in the solving of it. He suspected there were some, Detective Inspector George Bowman chief among them, who had envied him his disposition. Graves allowed himself a smile at the memory of his erstwhile companion.

'Gloucester Crescent!' The driver's announcement served to rouse Graves from his reverie. He was surprised at how quickly the journey had passed. Deep in thought as he had been, he had no memory of passing through Soho and Euston as he surely must have. Only the sweat on the horse's flank before him served as a testament to the distance and speed they must have travelled. With a nod of thanks, Graves swung open the wooden doors at his lap, leapt from the cab and turned his mind to the matter at hand.

The house before him was impressive. One of a terrace of smart townhouses, it rose over three floors from a tidy front garden planted with delphiniums and hollyhocks. A little path led to a front door flanked by a pair of plain, Doric columns. Each of the windows, Graves could see from the pavement, was hung with heavy drapes. They barely moved in the breeze that drifted lazily through the half-open casements. It was, mused Graves, an unremarkable scene. What was not quite so unremarkable, however, was the keening sound of a woman's cries that greeted him as he stepped through the little wrought iron gate from the roadside. As the driver cracked his whip behind him and the hansom retreated up Wellington Street, Graves took a breath, smoothed his curls with a hand and knocked at the door. In just a few moments, it swung open to reveal a severe looking footman in formal attire. His expression, however, was quite at odds with the neatness of his dress. Where his coat was pristine to the point of perfection, so his face was crumpled and lined. Where his starched collar and tie were neat to the point of fastidiousness, so his eyes were baggy and heavy with age. Despite all this, Graves noted a certain nobility about his bearing as he might expect to see in one who had spent a lifetime in service.

'Yes?' the man croaked. It was clear he was, or had lately been, in some distress.

'I am Detective Sergeant Graves of Scotland Yard.'

The footman looked the sergeant up and down.

'Are you alone?' He looked over Graves' shoulder as he spoke, clearly in hopes of seeing an officer more struck in years.

'Yes,' Graves offered cheerfully. 'Just me.'

Just as it seemed likely the man was to dismiss him on the grounds of his being too young to be taken seriously, Graves was taken aback to hear a shout from within the house.

'Let the man in, Bates!'

The old man turned back into the house with an audible sigh and led Graves through the entrance hall. As far as Graves could tell, it was a tastefully decorated house. The tiled floor had been lacquered to a shine. A hat stand stood by the door, although the footman made no effort to relieve Graves of his jacket. A large painting hung on the wall to the sergeant's right; a dark and forbidding pastoral scene that seemed to mix the architecture of a ruined Greek temple with a typically English landscape. In the centre of the picture, a half naked woman buried her face in the crook of her arm at the sight of a dead man at her feet. On the horizon, a stag reared upon its hind legs. The meaning, if indeed there was one, was quite lost on Graves as he followed the footman into the parlour to the front of the house.

'Detective Sergeant Graves of Scotland Yard,' Bates announced haughtily and Graves lifted his eyes to take in the room.

A fireplace dominated one wall, with a large mirror hung above it. Two tall, silver candlesticks stood at either end of the mantel, with a bust in between in the likeness of some ancient philosopher. To the back of the room, standing in the light of a side window, a small Queen Anne chair was placed near to a writing bureau. Neat piles of correspondence lay on its surface together with a collection of pens arranged in a holder around an ink well. More pastoral scenes hung from the walls so that barely an inch of wallpaper could be seen. Where it was allowed to show itself, Graves could see it was a deep flock fabric which, together with the heavy floral drapes at the windows, lent the room a luxurious air.

A smart chaise longue was positioned beneath the large window to the front of the house and it was upon this that the lady of the house was arranged, the very picture of grief. She took great gulps of air as she sobbed and her eyes were wet with tears. Her skirts billowed about her as she rocked back and forth in her agony, her face a mask of tortured anguish. Her maid fussed about her like a large, bothersome insect, a damp handkerchief in one hand and a bottle of smelling salts in the other. Graves could tell that, had it not been for her attendance upon her employer, she might well have given way to a similar grief. As it was, she offered such soothing words as she could in an effort to cajole her mistress. Graves took a breath. The very air seemed heavy with sorrow.

'I am Doctor Roger Curran,' came a voice, 'I can only hope you have a wisdom beyond your years.'

Sergeant Graves turned to see a man of middling stature and a large set of mutton chops. He was watching Graves carefully through suspicious eyes, as one might regard an unpredictable child. He had rested a slender hand upon the mantel in an effort to appear aloof from proceedings, though Graves could not help but notice the man's fingers drumming restlessly upon the dark wood as he spoke.

The man turned his gaze upon the woman at the window.

'This is my wife,' he announced, 'Mrs Jean Curran.'

His introduction was greeted with another heavy sob and Jean Curran's whole body shook where she sat.

'Will you attend to her, Abbie?' the doctor commanded, a note of impatience in his voice. The poor maid jumped at the sound and busied herself with kerchief and bottle. Mrs Curran waved her away.

'You must find my baby!' she keened, her hands held out to Graves imploringly. 'My baby's gone.'

'But that's just what the man has come to do, my sweet,' the man at the mantel said. He turned to regard the sergeant once more. 'We must simply trust that Scotland Yard has sent us their best man.'

'You may rely upon it,' Graves said, instantly regretting the smile that he had chosen to accompany the remark. Clearing his throat, he continued in more sober vein. 'May I know the circumstances of her disappearance?'

The words were barely out of his mouth before there came another cry of despair from the chaise longue.

'My daughter, Sergeant Graves,' bawled Jean Curran, quite uninhibited in her grief, 'My daughter has been taken!'

Graves reached almost instinctively for the notebook and stubby pencil he kept in his waistcoat pocket. Sensing the woman was too distraught to speak, he turned to the doctor.

'Might I know more?'

'Please,' said the woman, 'Won't you sit?' It was clear that she was making a tremendous effort to calm herself. 'Tea, Abbie,' she said suddenly. 'We must drink tea. And be sure to bring a cup for the sergeant.'

'Yes ma'am.' Abbie bobbed slightly in deference to her mistress. 'Shall I leave you with the smelling salts?' Mrs Curran took the bottle in her hands with a nod, and the maid left the room, a flush upon her cheeks. As soon as she was through the door, the lady of the house turned her attention to the young sergeant opposite. He had settled himself into the chair by the writing desk, conscious of being sized up by Doctor Curran as he sat.

'I will be brief,' she began, smoothing her skirts about her on the chaise longue, 'The quicker that you may begin the search for my daughter.' Graves nodded, his pencil poised. 'Rebecca is an imaginative girl,' Graves noticed the doctor roll his eyes at the mantelpiece, 'And always has been. But Abbie there seems to have the measure of her.' She nodded towards the door. 'She is the only one able to calm her in the mornings enough to get her to school. She gives her breakfast at seven of the clock, washes and dresses her, hears her tables for half an hour, then walks her to Hartland Road in time for her school day. It is a regular routine that suits them well.'

Graves nodded. 'And was such a routine followed this morning?'

'It was,' the doctor intervened from the fireplace. 'For all we know.' Graves couldn't help but raise his eyebrows.

'We are not early risers, Sergeant Graves,' Jean clarified, 'And do not tend to leave our beds until Rebecca has left the house.'

A sudden, heavy silence hung in the air as if certain words had been left unspoken.

Graves cleared his throat, suddenly awkward. 'But you saw your maid return?'

'We did,' the doctor retorted, 'At her usual time with provisions for the day.'

'Then the morning proceeded as expected?'

'So far, sergeant, yes.' Graves could tell Mrs Curran was struggling. She raised her handkerchief to her face, but not before Graves saw her lower lip begin to quiver with emotion.

'You should know, sergeant,' the doctor interjected, 'That I

19

run a consultation room directly above this room in my capacity as a General Practitioner.' Graves scratched feverishly at his notebook in response. 'At around ten o'clock I was seeing a patient, when there came a caller at the house. The door was answered by Bates, my footman.' Graves nodded. He wondered if this previous caller had been afforded more civility.

'I was seated here at the time,' Jean blinked, suddenly aware that she had not moved from her place on the chaise longue all morning. Her hands reached to the rug beneath her feet from where she retrieved a wooden frame. 'I was about my cross stitch.'

The doctor coughed, pointedly. 'I do not think the sergeant need be bothered with such details, Jean.' His wife dropped her gaze to her lap, chastened. 'Suffice it to say that the headmistress of the school, Mrs Beaufoy, was at the door. She claimed firstly that Rebecca had not come to school that morning and, secondly, this was not the first occasion.'

'But Abbie - ' Graves began.

'Swears she delivered Rebecca to the school gates as usual,' Mrs Curran concluded.

'And so I did.'

The small party in the room turned their eyes to the door. There stood Abbie, clearly stung by the insinuation, holding a tray of tea paraphernalia in her trembling hands. Clearly trying to retain some dignity as she walked, Abbie placed the tray on a small table by the chaise longue and proceeded to pour. Again, Graves noticed, the awkward silence had returned.

'How old is Rebecca?' he asked, simply.

Graves noticed the doctor look to his wife for confirmation.

'She will be eleven in two weeks' time,' Jean confirmed. This fact alone seemed to remind her of her dire position and, once more, she gave herself to her grief. Abbie dropped the teapot and ran to her mistress' side.

'Will you leave me be?' Jean sobbed in response. 'If you had taken greater care, she would be with us still.' Graves noticed Abbie bite her lip as she straightened up to respond. Just as she took a breath, he thought it best to intervene.

'What was Rebecca wearing this morning?'

There was another silence. As Graves looked between the two parents, it was clear that, having had no part in the girl's preparation for school, they did not know.

'She was in a navy blue pinafore,' chimed Abbie, 'And a straw hat with a red band was on her head.'

Graves pencil was almost a blur. 'Could you give a more full description of her?'

'She is tall for her age,' interjected Mrs Curran, feeling on safer ground, 'And uncommonly slender on account of her restless nature. She is never still, sergeant.' Hot tears sprang to her eyes as she spoke.

'She has chestnut hair to her shoulders,' added the doctor.

'Which she wore in ringlets this morning,' Abbie concluded. The Currans looked suddenly guilty, as if they were ashamed in their ignorance of such a detail.

'And you dropped her at the school gate?'

'As I always do,' the maid returned, pointedly.

'Did you see her enter the school buildings?'

Abbie shook her head. 'I did not,' she said, her voice almost a whisper. Jean Curran tutted from her place by the window.

'I had chores to be about, and I did not think she would go missing in the few short feet to the front door.'

'But that is exactly what happened!' Doctor Curran roared, suddenly agitated. 'Our daughter was in your care! Her welfare is your responsibility, as, I believe is her disappearance.'

Graves saw Abbie bite her lip again. This time, it was clear

21

she was holding back the tears. He felt sorry for her.

'Doctor Curran,' he began, 'You say you were with a patient when Miss Beaufoy called with the news of Rebecca's disappearance.'

'And so I was,' the doctor stuttered, clearly unused to being questioned so directly. 'Mrs Hampshire has been coming to me with stomach pains for some weeks.'

'So, she would be a witness to these proceedings?'

'You have witnesses enough,' he boomed, 'In the three people in this room. It happened just as we say, sergeant. Now,' he folded his arms in a gesture of defiance, 'What is Scotland Yard's finest going to do about it?'

Graves tapped his notebook with the stub of his pencil, deep in thought. 'You say this is not the first time Rebecca has gone missing from school.'

'So Miss Beaufoy would have us believe,' the doctor harrumphed.

'But you had no knowledge of any previous truancy?'

'Not until this morning.' It was clear Mrs Curran was keen to be of more help than her husband. 'Rebecca has been missing lessons of late. Miss Beaufoy says she was to talk to us of it in due course. I believe this morning was the last straw and she was keen for us to know the facts.'

'Where had Rebecca been going?'

Jean shook her head. 'No one knows. But she would always return in the afternoon, full of stories of her day at school.'

'Stories would be the right word for them,' concurred the doctor, 'Works of fiction.'

'Then what is to say,' offered Graves brightly, 'That she won't return, as usual, to the house this afternoon?'

Doctor Curran walked silently to the writing bureau. Bending to retrieve something from an inside shelf, he turned dramatically and held out his hand.

'This,' he said, simply.

Sergeant Graves moved closer. There in his palm, the doctor held a stone, a piece of string and a scrap of paper.

'This was thrown through our open window just as Miss Beaufoy was delivering the news of Rebecca's disappearance. Bates had shown her through to the parlour and she was sitting on the chair here at the bureau. My wife was on the chaise longue where you see her now but, luckily a little further to her left. Had she been but a foot to her right, the stone would surely have hit her. It was at that point that we thought it best to contact Scotland Yard.'

'You did not see who threw it?'

The doctor sighed with barely disguised exasperation. 'If we had, Sergeant Graves, do you think we should have withheld the information for so long?'

Graves had taken the note from the doctor's hand and was unfolding it with care, the better to read the message written there. 'I consider this the most pertinent piece of evidence we have concerning my daughter's whereabouts,' the doctor added, slyly, 'I should be interested to hear your thoughts.'

Graves angled the paper towards the light from the side window. There, written in a neat cursive style, were the words, 'Five pounds will set her free. Leave at the fire hydrant on Leybourne Road, four o'clock.' The message was written in a blue ink, Graves noted, with each word carefully placed at an equal distance from each other.

'Five pounds,' the sergeant muttered. There were paintings on the walls about him, he mused, that must be worth far more.

'A poultry sum,' barked Doctor Curran as he replaced the stone on the bureau.

Graves nodded. Though he would struggle to earn five pounds in a week as a detective sergeant, he had no doubt it was a poultry sum indeed to a doctor.

'Such a value he places on the life of our only child,' Jean Curran sniffed into her handkerchief.

'Should we pay the ransom, Sergeant Graves?' Graves noticed the doctor's fingers drumming on the top of the bureau in agitation. Glancing to the ornate clock on the wall above him, he saw it was almost midday.

'Perhaps,' Graves nodded, 'But we have four hours until the appointed time.'

'Will you find her in four hours?' The lady of the house was regarding Graves with imploring eyes. The sergeant dared not break her gaze.

'Mrs Curran, I will do all in my power to find your daughter.'

'Alone?' the doctor scoffed.

Graves let the challenge hang in the air. 'Doctor Curran,' he said at last, 'You mentioned Miss Beaufoy was here when the stone was thrown through the window. How long did she stay afterwards?'

'For a few minutes only,' the doctor replied, 'She was keen to return to her charges at the school.'

Graves nodded, tucking the message between the pages of his notebook. 'Then that is where I shall begin my investigations,' he said, brightly. He conjured up as winning a smile as was possible in the circumstances and turned all his charm upon the doctor. 'You may rest assured that I will do all in my power to find your daughter.'

The doctor nodded solemnly, but Sergeant Graves could not help but notice that the sound of his fingers drumming on the bureau   had   increased.

The sun was at its height as Bates showed Sergeant Graves to the door. He had been given to understand the school was but a five minute walk away on Hartland Road. Pressing his hand to his waistcoat pocket where he had placed the kidnapper's note, Graves mulled over the details of the case as he walked. If Rebecca was a persistent truant, she might well have made herself an easy target. Had she attracted unwanted attention as she wandered the streets of Camden? If the kidnapper knew her address and the class of person who might live in such a house, why had he asked for such a meagre sum to effect her release? A general practitioner of Doctor Curran's evident standing might command ten times that figure in a month. Why had the kidnapper not asked for more?

To his surprise, he was met at a junction by the Currans' maid, Abbie. She was clearly out of breath from running and must have taken a back way from Gloucester Crescent to as to meet with Graves unseen.

'Abbie?' enquired Graves gently.

'There's somethin' else, Sergeant Graves,' Abbie panted, attempting a curtsy that was almost comical. 'Something the Currans know nothing of. They'd have my guts for garters if they did.'

'Whatever is it?' Graves was all attention.

'A small thing, perhaps, but it would cost me dear if they knew.'

'I promise it will go no further.'

Abbie looked around her. Content she had neither been seen nor followed, she continued. 'Things have gone missing,' she whispered, conspiratorially.

Graves raised his eyebrows. 'Things?'

Abbie nodded, quickly. 'From the house, over the last two weeks or so.'

Graves could not help but be enthralled by the news, though he struggled to find a connection. 'What sort of things, Abbie?'

'That's the strange thing, sergeant. On their own, they're of no account at all, but together it's enough to have me out on my ear.'

'How so?'

'It started with odd bits of food,' Abbie rushed on, 'At first I thought I must be mad to lose it all about the place. Jars of jam and pickles at first, then half a loaf of bread and some smoked ham.'

'Are you sure it wasn't simply eaten by someone in the house?' Graves mused, 'Bates, perhaps?'

'So I thought at first, but he denied it when I asked him and he's not a man to tell fibs.'

Graves nodded, sure that he wasn't.

'But then, other things were taken. Strange things.' Graves leaned in closer to hear. 'A blanket first of all, from the girl's room. Then some of my mistress' favourite bone china plates. I've had the devil of a time concealing that, let me tell you.'

'Anything else?' Graves asked, aghast.

Abbie nodded. 'Some knives and forks,' she breathed, excitedly, 'Two of each. And a bottle of my homemade lemonade.'

Sergeant Graves narrowed his eyes in thought. 'You think it might be connected to Rebecca's disappearance?'

'Not for me to say, sir,' said Abbie, bobbing again. 'But if it turns out that way and I had said nothing, I should never have been able to live with myself.'

With that, the young maid looked around her once more. 'I must be gone before I am missed,' she concluded, gathering her apron about her.

'Of course,' Graves agreed. In truth, he liked Abbie. She had a manner about her that he found endearing. Pausing only to flash the sergeant a demure smile, the maid turned about and retreated quickly back the way she had come.

The young sergeant cast his eyes about him. Camden was not an area of London he knew well, and he had been surprised at just how genteel it appeared. Doctor Curran's house was just one of many that spoke of a certain professional reserve. Though not large, they were all well presented and maintained in smart rows along the street. Here, or at least along the roads immediately surrounding Gloucester Crescent, the professional classes were in abundance. Walking through James Street onto Chalk Farm Road, the casual observer would not have believed there was any inequality at all to be seen in the streets of the capital. Well-scrubbed doorsteps and smart carriages spoke of a certain pride at having reached a particular place in society. The busy roads were nonetheless clean and passable and the gardens uniformly smart.

Crossing the Regent's Canal on Hampstead Road Bridge, however, Graves could not help but be struck by a discernible difference in his environs. Suddenly, great wharves rose to his right while, to his left, the myriad tracks of the Midland Railway cross-crossed their way to the suburbs. Wherever there was a railway, Graves had learned, there was dirt. He didn't have to look too hard to see a sooty residue on the walls around him. The trackside was littered with debris, some of which had blown onto the road, which, even within the space of the hundred yards he had just walked, seemed suddenly less well-maintained. Even in the harsh, summer light, the alleys around him seemed suddenly dark and forbidding. The sun seemed that bit cooler. Pulling his collar about him, Graves picked his way across the street onto Grange Road. One more left turn, he knew, and he'd be at Hartland Road and Rebecca's school.

As he paused at the intersection with Leybourne Road, however, he noticed a commotion in progress. Panicked shouts echoed off the walls about him. Even against the backdrop of noise from the surrounding wharves and factories, he could plainly discern the name 'Jenny' being called again and again. From an alley on his right, Graves was suddenly confronted by a man of a very singular countenance. A main of jet-black hair was swept back from a widow's peak, his beady eyes scanning the roads about him for any sign of movement. A great, barrel chest protruded before him which, together with his beak of a nose and skinny legs gave him the appearance of a bird of prey.

'Jenny!' the man shouted again as he rounded the corner, nearly bowling into the sergeant. 'You'd better watch her step, friend,' he snarled as Graves pressed himself back to the wall.

'Who do you seek?' Graves pulled himself to his full height, determined to show no signs of being intimidated by the man's belligerent demeanour.

The strange man seemed to take a moment to consider the question, or at least if Graves was to be trusted with an answer.

'Good for nuthin' girl,' he rumbled, jamming the soggy stump of a cheroot between his teeth. 'About so high.' He indicated with his hand a height somewhere below chest height. 'Skinny bag o' bones with red hair and a sticky out nose.' He sniffed as he looked around him. 'Name of Jenny. Don't suppose you've seen hide or hair of such a one?'

Graves shook his head. It was clear that, despite his show of apparent hostility, the man's behaviour was born of agitation at the girl's disappearance. 'Who is she to you?' he enquired, gently.

'Daughter,' the man growled, 'Why, who are you to me?' He regarded Graves with suspicious eyes.

'Detective Sergeant Graves of Scotland Yard.'

His announcement caused a sudden change in the man. At once furtive, he took a step or two back into the road, struggling to find his voice.

'I've no need of a Scotland Yarder,' he said at last. 'She'll turn up in time.' Turning on his heels, the man called his daughter's name again, clearly making a show of avoiding the sergeant's gaze.

'How old is your daughter?'

The bird man stopped in his tracks, turning his head slightly. There was something in the tone of the young sergeant's voice that seemed to demand a response. 'Just shy of eleven,' he rasped. 'Why?'

Graves nodded, slowly. The coincidence, if coincidence it was, was too great to ignore.

'It would help a great deal,' he began, 'If I could know your name, sir. You have me at a disadvantage.'

'Evans,' the man growled reluctantly. There was something in the detective's manner he found almost unnervingly disarming. 'Peregrine Evans.'

Graves couldn't help but smile. It seemed entirely appropriate that the man before him should be named after a bird of prey.

'And when did you last see your daughter?'

The narrowboat had been moored some distance from the lock, half way between the gates and Hampstead Road Bridge across which Graves had walked just minutes before.

'That's my boat,' Evans was explaining, "It's Jenny's job to lead the horse.'

Graves turned his gaze on the old nag beside him. It stood, tethered to a water pump, seemingly quite content to munch at the little patch of weeds that grew where the water dripped from the standpipe. 'We were at work upon the gates when the girl went missing.'

Graves turned to see the lock-keeper had joined them. 'I've been looking around the coal yard next door,' he explained, 'To no avail.' He jerked a thumb over his shoulder to indicate the piles of coal that lay beyond a ramshackle old fence behind him.

'You have only looked this side of the canal?'

The lock-keeper seemed stung by the insinuation. 'So far.'

'There's no other way to cross the canal at this point than by the bridge,' Evans mused. 'We had not thought to look that far afield.'

Graves looked around the lock. As with much in the immediate vicinity, it had clearly seen better days. The canal banks were in want of maintenance, the lock gates in need of a coat of paint and the old lock-keeper's cottage in need of demolition. He noticed a line of weeds along the cottage walls, flattened where an old board was hung in place of a door.

'At what time did you notice she had gone?'

'At nine of the clock,' the lock-keeper replied, 'By my fob watch at least.'

The similarities in the case were striking. Graves removed his notebook from a pocket and licked the stub of his pencil.

'You'll not find her in the pages of your notebook, sergeant,' Evans sneered. 'We need men to search for her.'

Graves nodded, thoughtfully, his blue eyes twinkling in the light reflected on the canal.

'Mr Evans,' he soothed, 'Might I see inside your boat?'

Evans shifted awkwardly where he stood. 'To what end?'

'I would see where Jenny lived, that is all. It might help me build a picture of the child.'

'To what end?' Evans repeated, louder.

Graves sighed. 'Mr Evans, I have spent the best part of the morning in the company of a family stricken with grief at the disappearance of their daughter.' Evans' black eyebrows rose at the news. 'Like Jenny, she was just shy of eleven years old. And, like Jenny, she was taken at around nine of the clock this morning, when the maid of the house left her at school just a minute's walk from here.' Graves let his words sink in. 'It would be of tremendous use to me to know in what other ways these two cases are linked, for linked I believe they are.'

A silence hung between the three men as the import in the sergeant's words hit home. Then, suddenly and wordlessly, Evans turned and loped along the river bank to where his boat had been moored. 'Well?' he called over his shoulder, 'You comin' or not?'

Graves was struck by the sense of gloom about the place. As he descended the few steps from the wheelhouse to the living quarters below, it was possible for the sergeant to believe he was entering another world entirely. It was a world where space was clearly at a premium. Makeshift shelves were stacked with greasy tools and implements. Coils of rope littered the floor which, in turn, seemed slick with an oily veneer.

As he turned to speak to his companion, Graves noticed Evans dart to a corner even darker than the rest of the room. There he fumbled with an old blanket, endeavouring to cover a small box before Graves could notice.

'Mr Evans,' Graves smiled, 'I am not interested in whatever contraband you might be transporting from one end of the country to another.' Evans looked guilty beneath the sergeant's gaze. 'At least not today.' The sergeant looked around the confined quarters. What little light that was admitted through the dirty cabin windows seemed barely able to penetrate a few feet into the gloom. 'What were Jenny's duties?' he asked simply.

'The most important of all,' Evans explained, 'To lead the horse and thus the boat. To tend to him and keep him well.'

'Is she schooled?'

Evans sensed a trap. He knew it was now the law that education should be provided for canal children.

'She is schooled in the ways of the world,' he said, carefully.

In truth, Evans could not afford to have his child removed from her duties for the purposes of book learning.

'Is it like her to disappear in this way?'

'Not at all,' the boatman roared, 'She'd get what for if she made a habit of it.'

Graves let the comment pass. 'How often do you pass through the lock?'

Evans let the air whistle through his teeth. 'Three, four times a week. Depends on the cargo and the destination.'

'What do you carry?'

'Timber, like today,' the boatman grumbled, 'Coal, too. Sometimes ice for the big houses in the country, sometimes iron for the railways.' He snorted at the irony. 'I know, I know,' he cackled, 'It's like banging a nail in me own coffin.'

Graves frowned, uncomprehending.

'Here's me carrying timber for a new station near Aylesbury,' Evans explained, 'So the railways can do my job for me.'

'The railways are changing everything,' Graves concurred.

'And we are losing much as a result,' the boatman said.

Graves regarded his companion in the silence. There was a sadness about him that he had not noticed before; an awareness that Evans was perhaps the last of his kind.

'This boat has been in my family for three generations,' Evans continued, wistfully, as if aware of the sergeant's thoughts. 'I dare say there won't be a fourth.'

'I'll find your daughter yet,' soothed Graves, not entirely convinced by his own words. 'I believe your case and that of the Currans are connected. Find one daughter, find them both.'

'I should hope so,' replied Evans, 'I can't move without her. This little game is costing me dear.'

For the first time, Graves considered the girl's disappearance was more of a financial tragedy to the boatman than a personal one. Suddenly keen to feel the sun on his face once more, the sergeant turned to the steps that led back up to the wheelhouse. As he did so, however, his eye fell upon a pile of tattered blankets that lay, dishevelled, in a small cot in the corner.

'Is that where Jenny sleeps?' he asked, squinting into the gloom at what he felt certain was a familiar sight.

Evans nodded. 'What of it?'

Graves suddenly lurched for the cot, flinging the blankets to one side in a frenzy of activity.

'There'll be no finding her there, man,' Evans shouted in exasperation, 'Do you think I haven't searched the boat for her?'

'Not well enough, it seems,' Graves responded, a note of triumph in his voice. Holding his hand before him, he uncurled his fingers to reveal a familiar-looking piece of paper.

'What the Devil - ?' Evans began.

'This, Mr Evans, is the evidence I need.'

'Evidence of what?'

'That your daughter's disappearance is connected to that of Rebecca Curran.' He unfolded the note and held it up to the meagre light afforded by the cabin windows. It was written in the same neat, cursive style on a similar paper.

'Five pounds will set her free,' he read, excitedly, 'Leave at the fire hydrant on Leybourne Road, four o'clock.' It was exactly as had been written on the note thrown through the Currans' window that morning.

'A ransom?' Evans seethed.

'Do you have the money?'

Graves' question hung awkwardly in the air. The sergeant frowned. 'Mr Evans,' he repeated, 'Do you have the money?' He noticed Evans' eyes flick to a corner of the cabin, the corner where Graves had seen him fumbling furtively as they had descended the steps.

'French cigarettes,' Evans said, suddenly. Graves raised his eyebrows. 'In the box,' the boatman continued, a note of humility in his voice. 'I sell them where I can.'

Graves nodded in sudden understanding. 'And do you pay duty on the proceeds?'

Evans puffed out his already considerable chest in defiance. 'I have mouths to feed, Sergeant Graves.' He shuffled from foot to foot, suddenly awkward.

Graves looked around the cramped cabin again. It struck him that, for all that an outdoor existence might seem something to be desired, the life of a boatman must be a hard one. He turned to Evans. 'As I said before, Mr Evans,' he twinkled, 'I am not interested in that today.' Evans breathed an audible sigh of relief as Graves continued. 'Has anyone else had access to your boat since Jenny disappeared?'

'Not so far as I know,' Evans blustered, 'I've been searching the streets with the lock-keeper.'

Graves took a moment to think. 'Was he always in your sight as you searched?'

'No,' Evans said, slowly, 'But always within my hearing.'

Graves remembered the calls he had heard as he crossed Hampstead Road Bridge. There had, indeed, been two voices.

'Then who might have left this note?' the sergeant mused to himself.

'Seems to me,' said the boatman as he pulled an old, cracked fob watch from his pocket, 'That you have just three hours to find out.'

'Of course I haven't seen her.'

'Do you often work this lock?' Graves was squinting into the sun as he spoke. The smell of the steam from the brewery across the canal assailed his nostrils. A sweet aroma, it wasn't entirely unpleasant.

'O'course,' the lock-keeper replied, 'I've worked just about every lock from the Limehouse Basin to Hampstead Road.'

'He was with me every moment,' said Evans with more than a note of impatience in his voice. 'Jenny was with the horse as we opened the gates, then she was gone. It can't be laid at this man's door.'

'Did Jenny have any friends?'

'She 'ad no time for friends,' Evans growled, incredulous. 'Save the girl she'd meet here on the odd day we passed through. Similar age they are, though I can't see they had much else in common.'

'Seems Scotland Yard is at a loss,' the lock-keeper scoffed, folding his arms across his chest. Graves ignored the remark, confident the next steps in his investigation were becoming clear. Just as he turned from the lock, a sudden thought occurred to him.

'Mr Evans,' he began, 'Could you tell me if anything has gone missing from your boat over the previous few days?'

'Missing?' Evans was chewing on the stump of his cheroot.

'Small things,' Graves nodded, 'That might, at first, appear to be of no consequence?'

Evans scratched at his chin with his fingers. Graves noticed the nails were untrimmed and dirty. 'Well, I suppose…' the boatman mused.

'Yes?' Graves took a step nearer, his notebook already in his hand.

'We ain't got much between us, sergeant, Jenny and I.' Evans cast his eye over Graves' fine waistcoat and cravat. 'All we have is kept on the boat, so it's plain when things go missing.'

Graves felt his heart beat just that little bit faster. 'Such as?'

'Just last week, I noticed a bundle of candles had gone.'

'Candles?' Graves scratched at his notebook.

'I keep a few on the shelf for the darker evenings. Maybe five or six of 'em had gone. Thought I was goin' mad.'

Graves couldn't help but smile. He had heard a similar sentiment from the Currans' maid just an hour or so before. He was often amused at how people would more readily question their own wits than the evidence before them.

'Then two days ago,' the gruff boatman continued, 'Last time we passed through Hawley Lock, I noticed Jenny's doll had disappeared.'

Graves heard the lock-keeper sniggering behind him.

'It was given her by her mother,' Evans explained in his defence. 'It's all she has of her now. A knitted thing, like a cherub.'

'Did Jenny notice it's having disappeared?'

'No,' Evans shook his head, 'And that's the strangest thing of all. When I told her it had gone, she seemed not in the slightest bit concerned. Yet, ordinarily, she could not sleep without it.'

'Thank you, Mr Evans,' said Graves, stabbing at the page with his pencil to make a full stop to his notes, 'That is most helpful.'

'Helpful?' boomed the lock-keeper, 'I cannot see how any of that will help to find this poor man's daughter.' He shook his head. 'It's coming to a pretty pass when such a one as you can rise through the ranks at Scotland Yard.' Graves watched as the man walked away. 'Come on,' he sneered to Evans, 'Let's raise a crowd and search the whole of Camden if we have to.' He led the boatman away from the lock to the alley where Graves had first run into him. 'We'll leave the detective sergeant to his notebook.'

Satisfied that he had gathered all the information he could, Graves slipped the second note between the pages of his notebook, snapped it shut and returned it to his waistcoat pocket. Nodding slowly to himself, he wished the two men well in their search for Jenny Evans, then turned his heels towards

Hartland Road and Rebecca Curran's school.

It was a typically forbidding building. As Graves rounded the corner from Leybourne Road, the school presented itself as a rather austere institution. Its high, red-brick walls seemed more in keeping with a prison than an institution of learning and the windows were surely too high for any child to see out. In deference to the signs placed over the two sets of gates set into the wall, Graves entered via the 'Boys' entrance. He was confronted with a small yard, unadorned save for a chalk pattern on the flagstones. From behind a barred window, he could hear the chanting of children as they recited their tables. A plain, unfurnished door was set into the farthest wall, its paint peeling in the harsh glare of the sun. Tugging at the bell pull that hung beside it, Graves' mind turned to his own school days. His experiences had not been as unhappy as some of his acquaintance, but still he experienced the almost preternatural dread of being presented before the headmistress as he stood before the door. He almost had to remind himself that he was now an adult and had nothing to fear from the encounter, least of all a rap across the knuckles with a ruler. His thoughts were interrupted by the appearance of a small, rodent-like woman at the door. Her buck teeth protruded from a face that looked freshly-scrubbed. Her hair was scraped back into a severe bun that had the effect of tightening the skin on her forehead. Indeed, marked Graves uncharitably, it pulled her eyebrows up so far that it gave the unfortunate woman an expression of perpetual surprise.

'Yes?' she enquired with a voice that demanded to be listened to.

Graves swallowed. 'Detective Sergeant Graves of Scotland Yard,' he began by way of introduction. 'I wish to speak to Mrs Beaufoy regarding the disappearance of Rebecca Curran this morning.'

The woman looked about her, suddenly worried. 'I would ask you to lower your voice in the vicinity of the children when you speak of it,' she pleaded, 'I would not have their day disrupted any further.'

'Of course,' Graves demurred.

'In that case, you may come through to my office.'

With a start, Graves realised he was talking with Miss Beaufoy herself. He allowed himself to be led through a bare corridor that smelled of carbolic.

'We are a small school, sergeant,' Miss Beaufoy was intoning as she walked, 'With twelve boys and twenty girls. Gossip travels fast.' She opened the door to her office, a plain room with no consideration given to comfort. It comprised a single desk, two simple chairs and an entire wall given over to shelves groaning with paperwork. 'They have, of course, noticed that Rebecca is not with us today. I would not wish them to know of any investigation by Scotland Yard.'

Graves nodded. He noticed that Miss Beaufoy had no intention to sit but, instead, stood behind her desk, imperious. She gave the impression that she had a thousand things awaiting her attention that morning and would really rather she was left alone to attend to them.

'I understand you visited the Currans this morning.'

'That is so,' Miss Beaufoy replied, curtly. Scanning the shelves before her, she reached up to retrieve a particular record book marked, 'Attendances, Girls'.

'As you can see,' she began as she flipped through the pages on her desk, 'Rebecca's attendance can only be described as erratic.'

Graves leaned in to see where Miss Beaufoy was indicating with a slender finger. He saw a table of attendances; a list of twenty names or so filled a column to the left of the page with more columns of dates spread across the two open leaves. Each name was ticked under each date, stretching back two weeks. Graves located Rebecca's name and saw that, indeed, many days were left blank.

'We take a register every morning and afternoon,' Miss Beaufoy explained, 'Rebecca has rarely been with us for a full day.'

'Yet the Currans' maid swears she leaves Rebecca at the school gates every morning.'

'I am sure she does, sergeant,' the woman snapped, 'But that does not mean she goes through them.'

'Do you know where she goes?'

'We have employment enough keeping watch over the children within our school walls, let alone those who chose to spend their time without.' Miss Beaufoy crossed her arms defensively.

'Of course,' Graves nodded, eager to defuse the tension in the little room.

Miss Beaufoy relented a little. 'Word has reached us that she spends her time at the lock.'

'But why did you leave it so long before you notified her parents of her absences?'

Miss Beaufoy closed the book with a snap. Forcing Graves to take a step back to clear her way, she walked stiffly to the shelves and placed the book back in its place.

'An efficient school operates by a system of rules, Sergeant Graves, both within the classroom and in the office.' Miss Beaufoy pursed her lips. 'Rebecca Curran has been subject to a regime of punishments.' Graves shivered at the thought. 'None of which have worked. Our final recourse is to inform the parents so that they may punish her as they feel fit.'

'And if that doesn't work?'

'Exclusion,' said Miss Beaufoy, simply. 'Education is not a

right, detective sergeant.'

Graves nodded, solemnly.

'Rebecca Curran is a difficult girl,' Miss Beaufoy added. 'Given to day dreams and lapses in concentration.'

'Her own mother called her imaginative,' Graves concurred, remembering the conversation in the Currans' parlour.

'She is subject to continual fantasies. We do our best to smother her natural spark as we do with all our children. There is no room in the world for fanciful notions, sergeant, particularly in young girls.'

Graves was sure the headmistress knew best. Turning to the shelves behind him, his eyes fell upon some sheaves of lined paper stacked neatly by the window.

'Is that some examples of your childrens' work?' he asked. There was something about the paper that gave him pause.

'It is,' the headmistress nodded. 'The younger children work with slate and chalk, the older with paper and ink.'

'May I see it?'

Graves was convinced the headmistress rolled her eyes in a display of impatience. Clearly coming to the conclusion that he would be gone the quicker if she acquiesced, Miss Beaufoy reached out to lift the papers to the table.

'These are the results of the girls' test of a week ago.'

'Did Rebecca take the test?'

Miss Beaufoy thumbed through the papers, each of which was marked with a girl's name.

'You are in luck, sergeant,' she said at last, 'It appears that Rebecca deigned to join us that afternoon.' Pulling a sheet of paper from the bundle, she slid it to the centre of the desk. Graves could clearly see a number of simple words written again and again with a neat hand in blue ink.

'Are all the children taught to write in such a style?'

'It is the standard cursive form,' Miss Beaufoy asserted,

'Unfussy and clear. I teach it to the girls myself.'

Graves turned swiftly to the diminutive headmistress before him. 'Would you say, Miss Beaufoy,' he began, pulling his notebook from his pocket, 'That these two notes were written by the same hand?' Graves slid the two ransom letters from between the pages of his notebook and placed them side by side with the piece of paper on the desk.

Sighing, Miss Beaufoy leaned in closer to see. 'Almost certainly,' she said. 'Yes. That is Rebecca's hand without a doubt.'

Graves nodded, a smile spreading slowly across his face. For the first time since the reporting of Rebecca's disappearance, he knew he should have no fear for her safety. If he was right, both she and Jenny Evans were in no danger at all.

Doctor Roger and Mrs Jean Curran were clearly feeling out of sorts. They had wanted Sergeant Graves to deliver his findings in the comfort of their parlour, but he had been adamant that it should not do. Instead, he had insisted they follow him back to Hawley Lock, mindful of the passing of time. It was now almost four o'clock, the appointed hour at which the Currans and Peregrine Evans must make payment to see their daughters again.

'Must I bring the money?' Doctor Curran had asked, breathlessly, as he prepared to leave the house.

'Indeed, no,' Graves had responded with a smile, his blue eyes dancing with the excitement of it all.

'How then shall we save Rebecca?' Mrs Curran had stood, wide-eyed, by the front door, a parasol hooked over an arm.

'You are assuming, Mrs Curran,' Graves replied enigmatically, 'That she needs saving at all!'

With that, he had breezed past them both, his lightness of step only serving to confuse the couple even more.

Now they stood, Mrs Curran sheltering beneath the shade of her umbrella, at the side of Hawley Lock, Peregrine Evans shifting uneasily at their side. It was unusual for him to find himself in such refined company, and he was unsure how he should comport himself. He settled on merely tugging at his cap in deference to the doctor's status and bobbing his head beneath his wife's startled gaze.

'Mr Evans has lost his daughter, too,' Graves was explaining in hushed tones, 'This morning, under similar circumstances, right down to the ransom note.' He handed the pieces of paper back to the Currans and Evans respectively, and they marvelled at the similarity.

'But all this only confirms they were taken by the same man,' blustered Doctor Curran.

'Might I ask you to lower your voice?' Graves asked. 'It is imperative we do not startle them.'

'Startle who?' Mrs Curran asked, a look of confusion on her face.

Graves raised his fingers to his lips. 'Mr Evans,' he began, 'Might I trouble you for the time?'

As the boatman reached to his waistcoat pocket with his talon fingers, Doctor Curran turned to his wife, incredulous at the sergeant's erratic behaviour. 'I do not think he is taking this seriously at all,' he muttered, irritably.

'On the contrary, doctor,' Graves beamed, 'I have never been so serious in my life.'

'It has just turned four of the clock,' Evans growled. As if in confirmation, a bell chimed the hour somewhere beyond the canal.

'We should have left the money!' Jean Curran keened. 'We

will never see our daughter again!'

'Shhh!' Graves demanded.

Doctor Curran cast his eyes towards Leybourne Road. He knew the fire hydrant where they had been commanded to leave the ransom was barely a hundred yards away.

'Now what?' grumbled Evans, awkwardly.

'Now,' Graves responded cheerfully, 'We wait.'

All was quiet. Even the hammering of tools in the surrounding factories seemed to cease. Only the lapping of the water in the canal could be heard. The little party stood, holding their breath in a state of collective anticipation. Their eyes searched each other and the buildings around them for any clue as to the sergeant's intentions. Then, suddenly, there came a noise. As one, the assembled party turned to face the dilapidated lock-keeper's cottage. A rasping, scraping sound was coming from the hoarding that covered the door.

'At first I was confused by the amount demanded in the notes,' Graves was explaining as the board was slowly swung aside by a small hand, 'But then I thought to put myself in the girls' way of thinking. Five pounds is a lot of money to an eleven year old, would you not agree?' All eyes were upon him, he noticed, and they were widening with disbelief at every word. 'Rebecca certainly knew her father could afford it, and Jenny had clearly seen the money you collect for your contraband.'

Evans shifted guiltily beneath the Currans' gaze. 'I have mouths to feed,' he muttered in his defence.

'The final clue was in the handwriting,' Graves added, his golden curls shining in the afternoon sun like a halo. 'The ransom notes were clearly written by Rebecca's hand. Miss Beaufoy showed me examples of her work at her school.'

'But why?' Mrs Curran asked suddenly, 'Why would Rebecca

43

do such a thing to us?'

'And my Jenny, too?' Evans snarled.

'Perhaps,' Graves responded dramatically, 'You should ask them yourselves.' Moving to one side, Graves allowed them an unhindered view of the old lock-keeper's cottage. There, standing by the makeshift door that had been fixed, in vain, to deter intruders, were two young girls; one with a profusion of chestnut ringlets to her shoulders, the other sporting a head of red hair and an over-large nose. The taller of the two wore her school uniform.

'Jenny!' Evans roared, 'What do you mean by this nonsense? You've put me a day behind schedule.'

'Rebecca!' Mrs Curran was crying as she walked towards her daughter, 'Why would you do such a thing?'

Glancing behind the girls, Doctor Curran could see they had made something of a den in the tumble-down cottage. An old knitted toy, like a cherub, sat propped up against a wall next to a handful of candles that lit the room. Scraps of food and dainty plates and cutlery had been placed on a blanket on the floor, as if for a tea party.

'I think you'll find those belong to you, Mrs Curran,' Graves beamed. 'And I think you'll find, Mr Evans, that Jenny herself left that note on her bed.'

Having stood dumbfounded at the sight of their parents before them, the two girls turned their gaze upon each other and promptly burst into tears.

'You might well cry now, my girl,' Doctor Curran boomed from where he stood, 'But it's as nothing to the sound you'll make later when you feel my hand upon you!' It was notable, thought Graves, that he had made no attempt to move to the girl.

'And you, Jenny, will be put to work all the harder.' Evans' face was a picture of wrath.

'Lead your own 'orse!' Jenny snapped between sobs, 'I'm

gonna live in a big house and be a maid!'

Evans' face dropped at the absurdity of it all. 'With what?'

'With the five pounds you got in your box!' Jenny screamed in defiance. 'That's enough to pay for a train somewhere.'

'And then what?' Evans demanded. Jenny fell quiet. She had clearly not thought it through.

'She has a child's notion of the world, Mr Evans,' Sergeant Graves intervened, softly, 'And does not know the complexities of the world.'

'And you Rebecca,' Mrs Curran was demanding, 'Why would you do this to us?'

'I'm not wanted at home or school,' she cried, wiping her nose on the back of a hand. 'You'd be better off without me. The five pounds was to pay for food for Jenny and me while we thought what next to do.'

'I'll give you what-next-to-do,' seethed Doctor Curran, marching towards the young girl and grabbing her by the arm.

'You leave her alone!' Jenny screamed, kicking at the doctor's shins, 'She's the only friend I got!'

With that, Evans grabbed his daughter by the ear and pulled her towards his boat. 'You'll learn to curb your temper, girl!' he hissed.

Mrs Curran turned to Sergeant Graves in the melee. 'How did you know they were in the cottage?' she asked, confused and impressed in equal measure.

'Take at the look at the patch of ground by the door,' he said, gesturing with his head. Following his gaze, Mrs Curran could see where a clump of weeds was growing in the shade of the wall. Just beneath where the makeshift door hung from a nail, she could plainly see a small crop of dandelions that had been trampled underfoot.

'If the lock-keeper's cottage had been abandoned,' breathed

Graves excitedly, 'Just who had been treading on those weeds?'

The Silver Cross was as busy as ever. As Detective Sergeant Anthony Graves stood nursing a tankard of ale at the bar, he could not help but let his eyes wander to the wing-backed, leather chair by the fireplace. Through the throng of eager patrons, he could see it was occupied by a plump labourer in a floppy felt hat and heavy jacket. The man looked up and met the sergeant's eye. Graves looked away, guiltily, his thoughts turning to happier times. He wondered if Inspector Bowman would ever again join him for a drink by the fire.

'Drinking alone, Sergeant Graves?'

Harris, the landlord, was suddenly by his side, an empty tray of glasses in his hands. He flicked a stray strand of hair from his face as he spoke. At this time of year, he seemed more tanned than ever, though Graves could not profess to having ever seen him go outside.

'Yes, Harris,' Graves replied slowly, 'Just me.' As he stared into the bottom of his tankard, he swilled the dregs and let his thoughts wander. He could not guess what might become of the two girls he had met that day, but he could not help having an admiration for them both. Certainly, they had been resourceful in their schemes. They had only sought to better their position in the world, however naively they had gone about it. For now, he knew, they might well have made things worse. Graves sighed and downed the last of his pint. With a tip of his head to Harris on his way out, the young detective sergeant made his way from the bar and into the evening light, his thoughts turning to the prospect of a good night's sleep and a new day in the morning.

THE CHISWICK ROBBERY

SEPTEMBER, 1892

'The worst thing about these trams,' mused Detective Inspector Ignatius Hicks as he fought to get comfortable on the wooden bench that served for a seat, 'is that they never stop where you want them to.'

'There's a stop a hundred yards ahead,' replied the man on the seat next to him, an elderly gentleman in a rather faded brocade coat. He smelt of damp and naphthalene.

'Then that's a hundred yards too far,' wheezed Hicks, unhappily. Puffing furiously at his pipe, the detective cast a beady eye at the passengers around him. They seemed to present a microcosm of the city itself. Towards the front of the tram, he could see a grubby young couple with a small child bouncing on his father's knee. Behind them, a businessman in a silk top hat and smart frock coat dangled his fingers playfully in front of the infant, his eyes twinkling as the child gurgled in response. Three rows back, a thick-set man in a torn shirt and tatty waistcoat rolled on his seat, clearly drunk. He was occasionally roused from his stupor by the tram rattling noisily over the points in the rails beneath, only to mumble incoherently and slip back into a drunken slumber. Hicks noticed he had a painful-looking bruise beneath his left eye. He doubted he had even paid his fare. The conductor, eager no doubt for a quiet day, simply passed the man by without pressing him to buy a ticket.

'He'll stay there all day if the conductors will let him,' the man sitting next to him pronounced, unbidden. 'He travels the length of the High Road sometimes a dozen times a day.'

'What marvels he must have seen,' Hicks muttered, disdainfully.

He let his gaze drift to the window. Chiswick High Road was a busy thoroughfare. Pedestrians, carriages and horses wove their way along its length from Stamford Brook to Kew, often, it seemed, risking life and limb to do so. Lined with shops and public houses of every size and description, the wide road, quite apart from being the main artery to deliver traffic to the west, was home to those who simply wanted to amble in the late summer sun. A fall of rain overnight had lent the road and the trees that grew beside it a silver sheen.

'Turnham Green!' announced the conductor from the front of the carriage. The two ponies at its helm stuttered to a slow halt, their rippling flanks twitching in their harnesses. Heaving himself from his seat, Hicks squeezed past his fellow passengers, his great girth taking up the whole aisle as he lumbered the length of the tram. Reserving a special look of distaste for the drunken man on the seat near the front, he grabbed a hold of the pole by the door and swung himself almost daintily onto the road. The bell rang behind him to indicate the tram was once more on the move and Hicks stepped quickly onto the pavement, swinging his arms in an almost comical effort to regain his balance. He muttered beneath his breath as the tram continued on its journey. Hicks remembered a time before the trams. For the last twenty years they had become synonymous with London life, even out here in the suburbs. They had brought their own problems with them, of course. Since the first horse tramway had begun rattling down Victoria Street, there had been complaints about the congestion they left in their wake. Their greatest proponent, the aptly named George Train, was even charged with breaking and injuring the Uxbridge Road in Eighteen Sixty One, due to the damage his trams had caused to the road surface. Now, it seemed, people had simply got used to them. Smoother and roomier than the usual hansoms and broughams, they were also cheaper. And therein, according to the likes of Inspector Hicks, lay the problem. At only a penny for a ticket, the trams proved an irresistible attraction to the lower classes, some of whom were simply intent on finding respite from the elements. They became notorious for being the transport of choice for drunks, waifs and ladies of ill repute. For one day only, Detective Inspector Ignatius Hicks had joined them. Finding the cab ranks empty at Hammersmith, he'd had no choice but to board the tram and take his seat with the hoi polloi.

Propping himself against the trunk of a tree to recover, Inspector Hicks took a moment to catch his breath. Had he been of a mind to look up, he might well have noticed the tips of the higher leaves beginning to succumb to autumn's charms.

The slender, Gothic spire of Christ Church rose before him. Positioned in the middle of the green, it seemed almost incongruous. Completed only a decade before, its high flint walls were most at odds with the architecture of the shops and buildings along the High Road, so that it seemed remote from the world entirely. In fact, as it reared from the flat, manicured lawns of Turnham Green, it reminded Hicks for all the world of a marooned hulk in a quiet sea. Turning his eyes from the vagrants that sheltered in the church's shade, Hicks crossed the road to walk back the way the tram had come and towards the police station he had passed just minutes before.

Hicks felt very much as if he had drawn the short straw. With Bowman indisposed and Sergeant Graves busier as a result, it had fallen to the portly inspector to investigate the report of a robbery in Chiswick. In truth, Graves had been evasive of late. Rumour had it he was now operating within the purview of the newly-promoted Detective Superintendent Callaghan. Hicks rubbed his beard. He had rather hoped he might spend the day at The Silver Cross. Passing a newspaper boy outside a public house, Hicks paused.

'Robbery in Chiswick!' the boy cried. He was dressed in a tatty coat that was ragged at the seams. His face shone with burnished dirt. 'Priceless heirloom stolen!' Hicks was amused to hear him pronounce the 'h' in heirloom. He doubted the boy even knew what it meant.

Reaching into his pocket for a penny, the inspector reasoned he might as well acquaint himself with the details.

'Paper for the big bloke?'

Hicks looked behind him.

'You, mate!' the boy laughed. 'Want a paper?'

Hicks was on the verge of cuffing him for his impertinence.

'Not from round 'ere are ya?' The lad narrowed his eyes, suspiciously.

'And what of it?' Hicks just wanted his paper.

'Didn't think you looked the sort.' The boy was obviously content to stand and chat all day. 'Right snooty lot round 'ere. Some of them got pots of money too.' He held up his newspaper. 'And some of them can't keep a hold of it!' He stabbed at the headline. 'How can somethin' be worth so much?'

Losing patience, Hicks snatched the paper from the boy's hand.

'Here on business?' the lad enquired.

'Something of the sort,' blustered Hicks, unsure quite what it had to do with him.

'Saw you get off the tram. Took you a while to get your bearings.'

'You were watching me?'

'I watch everyone!' the boy laughed, playfully. 'Never miss a trick. Did you see old man Barraclough? The drunk? He rides that tram up and down all day, then spends his nights with the Duke Of Sussex.'

Hicks raised his eyebrows. 'Is the Duke local?'

'It's a pub, mate! Round the back of the common.'

Hicks nodded. He could tell he was being taken for a fool.

'What's your name, lad?'

'Herbert Roundtree. Most people know me as Bert.'

The inspector smiled. Just as Herbert was sure the gentleman was going to join in with the jape, Hicks suddenly grabbed the boy by the collar. 'Well, Bert,' he hissed into his ear, 'I'd just as well you kept your opinions to yourself.'

Shaking himself free of Hicks' grip, Herbert Roundtree nodded in understanding.

'Fair enough,' he said, simply.

'I need no snooper to tell me what's what.' Hicks straightened his great coat about him. Even in the September heat, he would not be seen without it.

'Scotland Yarder, are ya?'

Hicks lunged for the boy again, clutching at his lapels. He loomed so close, Bert could smell the tobacco on the inspector's beard.

'I would thank you to keep that to yourself.' He looked about him as he spoke.

'Thought so. You look like you reckon you own the place.'

Hicks eyed the boy. He was standing his ground. He must have credit for that, at least. Letting the lad go, the bluff inspector took a draw from his pipe and plunged his hand into a pocket. Placing some change in the boy's grimy hand, Hicks blew a cloud of smoke into the youngster's face. He barely flinched. Hicks allowed himself a smile and walked away, shaking the newspaper open to read the headline.

Behind him, Herbert Roundtree bent to pick up another paper, certain he would see the fat man in the large coat again some time.

'Audacious Robbery!" the headline shouted. The editor of The Chiswick Herald clearly loved a sensation. Hicks read on as he walked up High Road towards Chiswick Police Station.

Like a large vessel upon the seas, other pedestrians thought it best to give him a wide berth. They parted before him as he sauntered up the middle of the pavement, oblivious to their looks of reproach. For a detective embarking upon an investigation, he was certainly drawing attention to himself. Infuriatingly for those on the pavement behind him, Hicks slowed his pace as he read the article in the Herald.

'Police were called to the residence of Mr Noah and Mrs Amelia Metternich at Devonhurst, Duke's Avenue, on Sunday morning following the discovery of a robbery overnight.' Hicks puffed on his pipe. 'Following attendance by Sergeant Springer of Chiswick Police Station, it was found that a rare and marvellous piece of jewellery had been taken. The Traubenpokal had been stolen from where it stood in the library. Investigations are now underway to ascertain just who might have taken the item and what their intent may be.'

Hicks had no idea what a 'Traubenpokal' might be. Helpfully, an artist's drawing of the missing artefact had been included below the text. The inspector squinted at the picture of a tall, highly-embossed cup. The stem was in the form of some figure or other, while the bowl of the cup appeared as a bunch of grapes. Hicks was nonplussed. For the life of him, he could not imagine why such a thing might be either valuable or desirable. It was hardly practical as a cup. Hicks folded the newspaper beneath his arm. He had no taste for the finer things in life and rather resented being called out to investigate the disappearance of a tankard. Mrs Metternich herself had requested the involvement of Scotland Yard. Hicks scratched at his great beard. Perhaps the local police force had been found wanting. Passing beyond Turnham Green, the path became more crowded and the road busier. People queued at a bank on the corner with Clifton Gardens. Hicks saw shopkeepers with leather bags of change mingling with businessmen and tradesmen. The saw of a local joinery works sang into the air. A gaggle of schoolchildren crossed the road to a Roman Catholic chapel, their flustered teacher trying desperately to steer them safely through the oncoming traffic.

Finally, Hicks found himself outside Chiswick Police Station. The walk had been just a few minutes, but the portly inspector was out of puff. His face was flushed red beneath his beard. Hicks swept the hat from his head and wiped the sweat from his brow with a sleeve.

The building before him was impressive, almost stately. Sat back from the road behind a railing fence, it was a solid building of red brick and white plaster that rose over two floors. A large bay window occupied almost the entirety of one side of the station, and Hicks could see two or three members of the Force lounging against a desk within. A plaster coat of arms stood upon a lintel over the door, giving the entrance a rather grand appearance. Chiswick, mused Hicks, seemed to think very highly of itself. Lifting his coat about his ankles, he heaved himself up the steps and let himself through the door.

'Detective Inspector Hicks, I presume?'

Turning to his left, Hicks noticed a young man advancing upon him. He was dressed in the regulation police uniform of a heavy woollen tunic with polished silver buttons and a high collar. Hicks saw his helmet resting on the desk behind him.

'I am Sergeant Springer.' Hicks shook his hand. He noticed the sergeant immediately wipe it on his trouser leg. 'Do you know Chiswick?' Springer had a face that was easily read. He seemed a keen young sort, thought Hicks. Green behind the ears.

'I have the measure of the place,' Hicks grumbled. He waved his Chiswick Herald in the policeman's face. 'And I have my measure of the case.'

'Then you're an admirer of my handiwork?'

Hicks looked beyond Sergeant Springer to see a wellcoiffured man in an ostentatious checked suit. A purple cravat was looped around his neck. He clearly fancied himself a proper gentleman but, upon closer inspection, Hicks could see the seams of his jacket shone with grease and errant strands of cotton stood out from the hems.

'This is Geraint Fernsby. Editor of the Chiswick Herald.' Hicks' eyebrows rose beneath the brim of his hat. The newspaperman seemed very at home at the police desk.

'I often work hand in hand with Sergeant Springer,' he explained. 'Suits him, suits the paper. And it certainly helps sell copy.'

'Mr Fernsby has been good enough to include an artist's drawing of the missing Traubenpokal in today's paper, as you will have seen.'

Hicks nodded. 'Very realistic,' he blustered.

'Are you familiar with Hans Petzolt, Inspector Hicks?' Fernsby clearly sensed the opportunity to have a little fun with the bluff inspector.

'Is he the chief suspect?' Hicks asked in all innocence. He regretted it at once. It was clear Sergeant Springer was doing his best to suppress a smile. Fernsby on the other hand, was making no such effort.

'Hans Petzolt is the master craftsman who fashioned the Traubenpokal. He was Nuremberg's most prominent silversmith in the sixteenth century.' Hicks puffed furiously on his pipe, very quickly filling the room with a noxious fug. 'But then, of course, you knew that, as he is profiled in full on page five of today's Chiswick Herald.' Fernsby retreated back to his pace at the desk and leaned against it. He was plainly very happy with the outcome of his introduction.

'I must admit, I had not yet read that far.' Hicks was seething.

'You must forgive Mr Fernsby,' Sergeant Springer was saying. 'We make it a habit here at Chiswick Police Station to acquaint ourselves with every detail that might prove pertinent in the pursuit of our enquiries.' He gently chided the newspaperman with a look. 'It is something of a competition between us.'

'But,' interjected Fernsby, 'it leads to clear results! A successful local police force and an interested readership.' Fernsby pointed through the great bow window to the bustling street beyond. 'There won't be many out there Inspector Hicks, who do not this morning know of Hans Petzolt and his remarkable Traubenpokal.'

'And yet,' Hicks began, 'finding herself in peril and the victim of a robbery, Mrs Metternich took it upon herself to call Scotland Yard.' He puffed out his chest in triumph. 'Perhaps she did not think the local force was up to it.'

Springer smiled broadly. 'I am happy to learn where I can, Inspector Hicks.' The inspector thought something else lay behind the smile. 'But there are other details to this case that led to Mrs Metterich calling upon The Yard. You will know soon enough.'

'Ah, then we are to go to Devonhurst?' Hicks was relieved to find he remembered the address from the newspaper article.

'At once.' Springer swept his helmet from the desk and called into a small ante-room beyond. 'Constable Turner! I am to take Inspector Hicks to the Metternich's.'

'Right you are,' came the response for the other room. 'Look and learn!'

There was a note of cynicism in the exhortation. Again, Hicks noticed Springer trying to hide a sneer. He called into the room. 'Perhaps you will talk Mr Fernsby through the affray outside The Duke Of Sussex this Saturday last? It might prove fruitful to get some descriptions into the Herald.'

Fernsby nodded his head in assent.

'Are we to catch a cab?' wheezed Hicks as they walked down

the steps. His short perambulation from the tram stop at Turnham Green had resulted in a cramp in his calves.

'Cab?' Springer seemed aghast at the idea. 'Of course not, inspector. We shall walk!'

In truth, Devonhurst was only half a mile away, but it took Inspector Hicks all of twenty minutes to traverse the distance. He looked about him at the smart townhouses as he sweated his way down Duke's Avenue.

'The professional classes are all around us, Inspector Hicks,' Springer was explaining. 'With the opening of the trams and the coming of the railway, it is easy enough for them to get to London and yet still not feel part of it. Doctors, bankers, architects and merchants all make their home in Chiswick. They soon make themselves the envy of others less fortunate.'

'Oh?' Hicks puffed.

'There is a class of man who, having made something of himself, will feel the need to show it.'

Hicks could see the sergeant was right. As he passed the neat houses beside him, he peered in at one or two of the windows. It took no effort at all to see the expensive trinkets on display. Large pictures hung on walls, shelves groaned with all manner of sculptures and jewellery and fine furniture filled every room. Occasionally, Hicks would catch sight of one of the house's residents, perhaps the lady of the house. Even at this early hour of the morning, they were dressed in their full finery. So much so, it would not have surprised Inspector Hicks in the least to see any one of them fix a sparkling tiara to her head.

'They're only going to the shops, or perhaps to volunteer at some chapel or other,' laughed Springer. 'You'd think they were meeting the Queen herself.'

Hicks could quite see how they might make themselves a target. 'Are the Metternichs known for their riches?' He was struggling to keep up with the lithe Sergeant.

Springer turned to his companion. 'I would wait and see, if I were you,' he teased.

Devonhurst stood alone in its plot on Duke's Avenue. A sweeping drive meandered from the road flanked by the leathery leaves of a yew hedge. A large cedar tree grew in the front garden, casting its shadow over the austere, three-storey house behind it. Indeed, Hicks wasn't certain if the front of the house would ever see the sun. Resting against the low wall on Duke's Avenue, he took advantage of an opportunity to both look the property over and rest his huge frame. He reached into his pocket to pull out his pipe, loosening the drawstring on his tobacco pouch as he looked around.

The house was double fronted, with two wings standing aside an impressive entrance hall. A flight of black and white tiled steps rose to a door that was glazed with coloured glass. Every window, Hicks noticed, was adorned with curtains that were drawn against the world. Holding his breath to listen, Hicks realised not a sound came from the place. Not a raised voice nor the sound of an instrument. There was no sign of a gardener nor of any activity either inside or out, for aught that he could see. It was quite possible to believe, mused the inspector as he drew gratefully on his pipe, that the house was devoid of occupants.

'How many people live here?' he asked Springer.

The sergeant stood with his hands in his pockets regarding the inspector with interest. 'Mr and Mrs Metternich and three staff are the sole occupants,' the sergeant elucidated. 'A footman, a maid of all work and a cook.'

Hicks' gaze had been drawn beyond the house to a tall palisade that ran the length of the garden's perimeter.

'What lies beyond that fence?'

'The gardens of The Royal Horticultural Society,' the

sergeant replied, breezily. 'It's much smaller than it was on account of them opening grounds in Kensington.' He looked at Hicks. 'I'm a bit of a gardener myself, inspector, so I take an interest.'

Hicks nodded, absently. 'And there?' He had lifted a heavy hand to point back up the road. The pitched roofs of several factories peered over a high wall.

'Paperworks,' replied Springer, 'and an Army and Navy Depository. The workers have all been questioned but noticed nothing out of the ordinary over the past few days.'

Hicks breathed deep to buy himself some time. The sergeant had certainly been thorough. 'Where did the thief gain entry?' he puffed.

'Ah,' replied Springer enigmatically. 'That is probably the most interesting detail of all.'

With that, he turned away from the road to walk towards the house, the gravel of the drive crunching beneath his boots. Hicks heaved himself from the wall and followed him. From his initial lack of enthusiasm at the case, Hicks had found some points of interest, not least the keen police sergeant himself. He seemed thorough, Hicks mused, and trustworthy too. He could not imagine a finer example of The Force to investigate such a crime. He instilled confidence. Which made it all the more puzzling why Mrs Metternich had called on Scotland Yard.

Sergeant Springer was by now some yards ahead. Hicks swung his arms wildly about him in an effort to keep up, but was surprised to see his colleague veer suddenly around the corner of the house, away from the entrance. Where the drive divided to the left and right, so Springer had headed right, around the back of the house. Hicks noticed a mischievous smile playing about the sergeant's lips. He ducked behind a row of outbuildings, gesturing that Hicks should follow him with an outstretched finger. As Hicks rounded the corner, he found

Springer standing in a patch of rough ground near the perimeter wall.

'Here's where the thief gained entry,' he explained, simply.

Hicks followed his gaze to the ground. He could see where the earth had been dug away to reveal a hatch in the ground; two wooden doors attached to hinges on a frame.

'A tunnel some twelve feet below the ground.'

'This leads to the house?' Hicks' eyebrows rose as he followed the imagined course of a tunnel towards the house.

'It emerges in the library, through a hatch in the hearth.'

Hicks tried to look thoughtful. 'Who knows of the existence of this hatch?'

'Ah,' said Springer again, laying a finger aside his nose. I wish the fellow would stop being so bally obtuse, thought Hicks. 'That's just it, inspector.' Just as Hicks thought he'd never get to the point, Springer continued. 'No one knew of the existence of this tunnel. Not the staff, not the groundskeeper, not Mr and Mrs Metternich themselves.'

'How on Earth could a groundskeeper work this garden and not know of its existence?'

The sergeant squatted on his haunches. Hicks declined to follow suit lest he couldn't get up again. 'These hatches were several inches below the earth. You can see how deep the thief had to dig just to get to them.'

Hicks nodded at the piles of earth on each side of the hole. The entrance to the tunnel lay a good eight inches below the level of the surrounding grass.

'How long has the groundskeeper been in service here?' Hicks asked.

The sergeant pulled a notebook from his pocket and leafed through its pages. 'Mr Knightly is employed on an ad hoc basis, as he is by many people in Chiswick with a garden to keep,' he summarised. 'He has been in place for the last two years, since the gardener was retired.'

'I suppose that's reasonable, then.' Hicks conceded. 'What was the purpose of the tunnel?'

'Nobody knows,' said Springer. 'It is certainly many centuries old, older than the present house itself. I can only surmise it served as an escape for the residents of the previous house.'

'Escape from what?' Hicks blustered.

'From whom, more like. The previous house dated from the civil war.' Springer looked around him. 'This whole area was Roundhead country, inspector. You have heard of the Battle Of Turnham Green, of course?' He knew full well he hadn't. Hicks nodded, nonetheless. 'Then you will know that the battle resulted in a standoff between the parliamentary forces and the King's supporters.'

'Of course,' Hicks swallowed.

'The Royalists were brutal.' Springer's voice had taken on a sombre tone, as if the events he was describing had happened only the day before. 'If I was of a parliamentary bent, I might well have constructed an escape from my house in case of an incursion.'

'But what is the point of the tunnel ending here? It surfaces in the grounds.' Hicks pointed at the perimeter wall that stood a good twelve feet further on. 'It would hardly give a man any advantage at all.' He knew at once that he had opened himself up to ridicule.

'The perimeter wall stood closer to the house, Inspector Hicks,' Springer said slowly, as if that would help Hicks understand. 'The original tunnel would have emerged well beyond it.'

The inspector sought to change the conversation at once.

'Shall we?' He gestured to the house.

Springer nodded. 'Of course.'

Hicks let the policeman lead the way again, back round to the front of the house and up the tiled steps. As he pulled at the bell, Hicks turned to look back out to the road. It would be easy enough to approach the house unseen at night. There were no gates at the drive. But just who would know of the hidden tunnel?

Hicks turned as he heard the door swing open on its hinges. He was greeted by a man taller and thinner than he had ever seen.

Sergeant Springer gave a cough. 'I have brought Detective Inspector Hicks from Scotland Yard.'

The footman gazed at the portly inspector.

Hicks shuffled uncomfortably beneath such scrutiny. 'I will offer every assistance, I am sure.'

'I should hope you will, Inspector Hicks,' came a clipped voice. 'Or there would be little point in you being here.'

The man had the complexion of one who seldom saw sunlight. His skin was translucent. Likewise, the delicate hands that curled around the door were pale as chalk. Hicks could plainly see blue-grey veins beneath the skin, threading their way across his wrists.

'Detective Inspector Hicks comes highly recommended,' Springer lied. Hicks fought to look worthy of so lofty a claim.

Fortunately, the footman felt convinced enough to let him in. 'I will not have that in the house, if you please.' He pointed to Hicks' pipe. Without a further word, he opened the door to its full extent and turned back into the house. Hicks tapped the bowl of his pipe against his heel to dislodge the tobacco. Sergeant Springer nodded approvingly and gestured that the inspector should enter the house before him.

Peering beyond the threshold, Hicks saw a long sideboard that ran the length of the hall. Only when he stepped in did he notice just what an impressive piece of furniture it was. It was of a dark wood that he took to be mahogany, and was inlaid with gold leaf around the edges, joints and drawers. More remarkable, however, was the collection of objet d'art that stood proudly upon its smooth surface. Hicks had never seen such a hoard of timepieces, all ticking quietly in their place. There were nautical clocks and carriage clocks of all sizes, each one more opulent than the last. There was a preponderance of gold, silver, garnets, diamonds and sapphires. Here there swung a pendulum, there a mechanical wheel spun feverishly to keep time. Just as Hicks opened his mouth to comment, he was interrupted by a chorus of chimes and bells to mark the quarter hour. The inspector turned to see Sergeant Springer twinkling beside him. He gestured to the wall above the sideboard and Hicks followed his gaze. There were at least half a dozen Old Masters, clearly all originals, leading the way to the parlour. Had he been conversant in such things, Hicks might have recognised the work of Alfonso Lombardi, Pedro de Mena and Matthias Stom. As it was, it was enough that he recognised that these few paintings alone would be worth an inestimable sum. As the men were led into the parlour, the footman stood aside to let them enter. They were greeted with further displays of finery. The most sumptuous furniture lined the walls. An elegant Chippendale display cabinet took up nearly the whole width of the room. Its unfussy, neo-classical design was the perfect medium by which to display the embarrassment of riches on its shelves. Porcelain sculptures competed for space with priceless vases. A whole shelf was given over to Chinese ceramics. As Hicks took in the rest of the room, he was suddenly aware his jaw was hanging slack. Snapping it shut, he took a breath to steady himself. Everything in the room, from the chandelier that hung from the ceiling to the Persian rug beneath his feet, was worth more money than he would ever see. He doubted a year's salary as a Detective Inspector at Scotland Yard would even buy him the candelabrum that sat upon the writing desk by the window.

'Mrs Metternich, good day.' Sergeant Springer introduced himself to a severe looking woman in a dress that came up to her neck and fell to her ankles. 'This is Inspector Hicks.'

'Charmed,' Hicks offered, sweeping his top hat from his head and attempting an obsequious bow. He knew at once it wasn't the most appropriate greeting.

'This is my husband, Mr Noah Metternich,' Mrs Metternich was saying. Inspector Hicks made an effort to regain his composure. He was quite aware that Sergeant Springer had been enjoying his reaction.

'I am Detective Inspector Hicks from - '

'Yes, yes, Scotland Yard, I know.'

Hicks couldn't help but look affronted. It was bad enough that the man behind the writing desk had interrupted him at his introduction. It was worse still that he had conspicuously refused to stand to present himself.

'Forgive my husband,' Mrs Metternich turned to the inspector. 'He has a natural suspicion of those in authority.'

Hicks was startled to realise she meant him. 'Might I ask, madam, just why you called upon The Yard?' Hicks cast a withering look to Sergeant Springer. 'Were the local police force not sufficient?'

As Mrs Metternich took a breath to respond, her husband interjected. 'They have certain connections of which I cannot approve.' He spoke in clipped, Teutonic tones. Hicks raised his eyebrows. Springer was suddenly subdued.

'My husband and I have led a blameless life inspector,' Mrs Metternich continued. 'At least as blameless as any other in Chiswick. Yet Mr Fernsby of The Herald will dig and dig until he hits gold. He'll find nothing, of course.'

Hicks tried to hide his confusion. 'Indeed?' How he wished he could smoke his pipe. He was missing the feel of the bit between his teeth as he thought.

'We care not for the Chiswick Herald,' announced Mr Metternich. 'Only for getting my Traubenpokal back.'

'Of course,' Hicks concurred. 'Might I know more of the circumstances under which it disappeared?'

'Disappeared?' Metternich was suddenly outraged. 'It was taken!' Throughout his burst of anger, Hicks noticed, he remained seated at his desk. There was much about the situation that perplexed him. Out of all the fine things in the house, why did the thief take the trouble to take the Traubenpokal?

'We were both asleep on Saturday night.' Mrs Metternich spoke calmly and carefully, but there was a weariness to her tale. Hicks had no doubt she had already recounted this story many times. 'I was woken at about midnight by a noise from the library.' Hicks would have taken out his notebook if he'd thought to bring one. As it was, he fought to commit the salient points to memory. 'The staff were obviously in their beds at so late an hour, so I reasoned we must have an intruder in the house. By the time I had reached the library, the intruder had gone the same way he had appeared, through the tunnel we have since discovered.'

Hicks raised his eyebrows in surprise. 'You risked confronting the intruder alone?' His tone betrayed his outrage. 'Surely your husband would be better placed to protect the household?' He shot a look at Mr Metternich.

There was a sudden silence in the room. Sergeant Springer cleared his throat. With a look of reproach, Noah Metternich dropped his hands from the writing desk. Hicks saw a flurry of movement, and Metternich wheeled himself into the room. With a pang of guilt, the inspector realised the man was an invalid. With both legs missing below the knee, his means of propulsion was the converted armchair on which he sat, a blanket covering his lap. A pair of out-sized wheels had been attached via an axle at either side. A smaller guiding wheel at the back kept balance. Metternich's hands danced over the wheel rims with practiced skill as he turned to the inspector.

'As you can see, Inspector Hicks, I am not the most effective deterrent.'

Hicks gulped. 'I see,' he mumbled, awkwardly.

'I had both my lower limbs detached four years ago.' It was a strange choice of words, thought Hicks. 'I have suffered with the diabetes for many years.'

Hicks nodded, sagely. He had heard of the condition, but he was blowed if he knew what it was. As if sensing his thoughts, Mr Metternich gave a wry smile. 'Do not trouble yourself, inspector. It is not contagious. But you can see why my wife came to the library alone?'

Mrs Metternich was looking suddenly unsure of herself. 'Inspector Hicks, I had hoped calling in Scotland Yard would be a good thing.'

'Of course,' said Hicks, stroking his beard in agitation. 'Might I see the room from which the object was taken?'

'Of course. Follow me.' Mrs Metternich turned back into the hall and led the men through a warren of corridors to the farthest side of the house. As they walked, Hicks took advantage of the time to ask Sergeant Springer for more details.

'Exactly what grievance does Mrs Metternich have against Mr Fernsby of The Herald?' he whispered.

Springer spoke out of the corner of his mouth, being careful that Mrs Metternich couldn't overhear. She strode ahead of them by several paces, a bustle of officiousness. 'Fernsby has long suspected the Metternichs of having come by their fortune by nefarious means.'

'What nefarious means?' Hicks spluttered.

'He had heard rumour of Metternich embezzling funds in Prussia, at the bank where he was president.'

'Was there any evidence?'

'None that Metternich could not refute, but the suspicion remains.'

'In my experience, Sergeant Springer,' opined Hicks grandly, 'there is no smoke without fire.' He tapped his finger on the side of his nose conspiratorially and gave a very obvious wink. Had Mrs Metternich turned at that moment, it would have been very clear to her that something was afoot between the two policemen.

'You do not subscribe to Sir William Garrow's assertion that a man is presumed innocent until proven guilty?'

'New-fangled nonsense,' Hicks grumbled.

'The idea is over a hundred years old!' spluttered Springer. 'I do not think you could call that new-fangled!'

Hicks declined to answer. He sensed there was a trap in everything Springer said and resolved to be more circumspect in his dealings with the man.

Mrs Metternich led them into a light and airy library. Tall windows gave out to a manicured lawn. The grass was neatly trimmed, the beds impeccably presented. Looking about him, Hicks saw shelf after shelf loaded with books of every size. He could tell they had been catalogued and arranged in some sort of order. Beyond that, each shelf was labelled in a stark, Germanic script; '*Geschichte*,' '*Philosophie*,' '*Volkswirtschaften der Welt*.' Hicks was none the wiser, but he could see it was quite a collection.

'There are many first editions among Noah's collection, inspector.' Mrs Metternich was standing with her hands clasped before her. 'That one beside you is perhaps worth a thousand pounds.'

Hicks had to resist the urge to whistle. The book looked innocuous enough; a brown leather-bound volume with gold inlay. There were several such books on the same shelf. Could they all be so valuable?

'My husband brought them with him from Prussia. You could say they are the closest we have ever got to having children.' There was a sudden sadness in her voice, but Mrs Metternich was too pragmatic a character to let it stay for long. 'But I did not bring you here to look at books.' She dropped her hand to point at the hearth. 'I brought you here to show you this.'

Hicks followed her finger down to the floor, to see the tiled hearth had been smashed. Broken shards lay in piles around the place, clearly indicating they had been smashed from beneath.

'So that was the noise you heard as you slept,' Hicks nodded, resisting the urge to reach for his pipe.

'Indeed, inspector. You can imagine my surprise at such a sight. At first I was so confused at the appearance of a tunnel under my house that I did not even notice the Traubenpokal had gone.'

'It was kept on the mantelpiece?'

Mrs Metternich nodded.

'How long did it take you to come to the library from your bedroom?'

Mrs Metternich thought. 'Perhaps seven or eight minutes.'

'Then the thief not only knew of the existence of the tunnel,' the inspector thought aloud. 'He also knew of the existence and whereabouts of the Traubenpokal.'

Hicks noticed Springer nodding as if to encourage a struggling student.

'Noah is very careful to always lock the library door at night.'

Mrs Metternich was pursing her lips.

'But, the windows?' Hicks had turned to look out to the lawn.

'The latches are thrown every night,' Mrs Metternich said, simply. 'There is no sign of them having been disturbed.'

Hicks harrumphed. Leaning against the window sill, he took a moment to review all he had learned. The thief had gained access to the house using a tunnel that no one had heard of. He had taken less than eight minutes to break through into the library, retrieve the Traubenpokal and make good his escape. Hicks puffed out his cheeks. His stomach rumbled in protest at his lack of a hearty breakfast. He placed a hand on his belly to quieten it, but fancied the assembled party had heard it anyway. 'Mrs Metternich,' he began, 'I have all I need for now.'

'You do not wish to question the staff?'

Hicks turned to see Mr Metternich had wheeled himself to the library door.

'There is no need,' Hicks boomed. 'I can see no reason why a member of your staff would leave the house at midnight, skirt around the house in the dark, dig through several inches of earth to the tunnel, then break through the hearth to gain access to the house. Surely, they might just as well have retrieved the key for the library door?'

Mrs Metternich nodded. There was clearly no faulting the inspector's logic.

'Of course, I interviewed the staff myself,' Springer interjected, ever the efficient police sergeant. 'I am happy to show you the results in my notebook.' He reached into the pocket of his tunic.

'I would prefer to investigate these matters in my own way,' Hicks blustered.

'The Scotland Yard way?' asked Mrs Metternich, hopefully.

'If you like, Mrs Metternich, yes.' Hicks puffed out his chest. Noah Metternich turned full circle in the doorway and wheeled himself from the room. 'Gott im Himmel,' he hissed under his breath.

Hicks drew gratefully on his pipe. In another month, these streets would be strewn with leaves, he mused as he puffed his way back up Duke's Avenue with the sergeant. The road was lined with London Plane trees, their broad leaves affording a good deal of shade from the low September sun. As Sergeant Springer had intimated in the grounds of Devonhurst, Chiswick was rich in history. How much of it, Hicks wondered to himself, had been presided over by these ancient trees?

Over a thousand years, Chiswick had grown from a humble village clustered for comfort around the local church, to a thriving and attractive hub for the middle classes. With them, as ever, came the sprawl. The well-to-do needed staff, and staff needed amenities. Those that were not resident with their employers required housing. The result was a booming population. Indeed, Chiswick had seen a tenfold increase in the populace in under a century. Suburban estates had been planned and built, and the ubiquitous rail network had provided connections to the west of London. The streets were busy with tradespeople and shopkeepers making deliveries. Passing a cart loaded with pies, Hicks' mind turned to where he might find sustenance.

Sergeant Springer pulled a fob watch from his pocket. 'But, it is only past a half past eleven,' he exclaimed.

'Then that is the perfect time to rest and think upon matters,' replied Hicks airily. 'Is there a public house within a short walk?'

Springer snapped his watch shut and gave the matter some consideration. 'I know just the place,' he said at last.

'Excellent,' said Hicks, relieved at the news. He had seen a number of taverns along the High Road. Any one of them would do. Suddenly, however, Springer changed direction.

'Where are you going?' wheezed Hicks, perplexed.

'The City Barge,' Springer called back. 'It's but a short walk, as you requested.'

Hicks' eyes narrowed. 'How short a walk?'

'Twenty minutes.' Springer was already increasing his pace, his long legs carrying him at speed away from Hicks. The inspector rolled his eyes, gathered his coat about him and set off in pursuit.

The riverside was already heaving with people. Stallholders had erected shabby stalls along the banks to sell their wares. Punts and boats were tied to their moorings. Even this far out of London, the river was busy. Barges laden with coal and wood sauntered past, sail boats angled their rigs to the wind. Small ferries carried passengers over the river, despite the presence of Kew Bridge barely a quarter of a mile away. The weight of traffic across its arches made it almost impassable to those on foot and so, despite it, the small rowboats that bobbed across the wide river thrived.

Short of breath from his exertions, Hicks rested upon a low wall by the river's edge. Sergeant Springer stood with his hands on his hips, nodding to those who he knew amongst the throng. Occasionally, he would resort to cuffing an urchin about the ear. 'Behave,' he cautioned one in particular who he had spied taking bread from a barrow. 'There's room enough in my cells, you know.' The young boy stuck out his tongue in defiance and ran barefoot through the crowds, no doubt intent upon trying his luck beyond the prying eye of the law.

The water was at its highest point of the day, lapping against the river wall. Hicks saw a small island halfway across the water.

'They say Oliver Cromwell himself took refuge there,'

Springer explained. 'It's known as Oli's Island as a result,' he chuckled.

Hicks nodded, thoughtfully. Springer was ever a man for details. Straining his eyes against the sun's reflection on the water, Hicks could just make out a small, makeshift jetty. A fishing rod lay propped up against it. 'What's the smoke?' Hicks pointed with the stem of his pipe to a haze that hung in the air above the island.

'That's the smithy,' Springer elucidated. 'Elias Cooper and his daughter are the only inhabitants. He guards their paradise jealously. But you can ask him about that yourself.'

''Ere, mister,' came a voice. 'You got any spare tobacco?'

Hicks looked down to see a young girl at his feet. She was dressed in a ragged smock and straw hat. She clutched an unlit pipe in her grubby hands.

A stern looking man was reaching after her. He had a harsh countenance and angry eyes. His skin was marked with pocks and scars. 'Lucy! Will you get back here? There's work to be done!' His hob-nailed boots skidded across the cobbles.

'Morning, Mr Cooper,' beamed Springer. 'Morning, Lucy.'

'Sorry to be botherin' you, Sergeant Springer,' said Cooper, reverently.

'Quite, alright, Mr Cooper.' Springer crouched down and held the girl by a shoulder. 'I am sure the detective inspector would happily share his tobacco.' He met Hicks' gaze. 'Wouldn't you, detective inspector?'

The girl's eyes widened so far Hicks was sure they would pop out of her head.

'He's a detective inspector?' Lucy stammered, far too loud for Hicks' liking. Cooper stopped dead in his tracks. People around them ceased their conversations and turned their heads.

Hicks fumbled for his tobacco pouch, suddenly aware of the eyes upon him. As he pinched some tobacco between his fingers, he saw Springer nodding encouragingly to the girl.

'He's come to investigate the little altercation at the Duke Of Sussex on Saturday night.' He cast a knowing look to her father. 'Would you happen to know anything about that, Mr Cooper?'

Hicks did his best to cover his confusion. What was Springer playing at?

'I saw nothin' out the ordinary, Sergeant Springer,' Cooper was mumbling. 'But here's always some as can't handle their drink.' He swallowed. 'Reckon things got a little out of hand, that's all.'

Springer held his gaze for a moment then whisked the hat from Lucy's head and tousled her hair. 'Have you got your fill, Lucy?'

The girl peered into the bowl of her pipe and nodded. 'Then be on your way and keep your old man out of trouble.'

Striking a match on the heel of her shoe, she took a puff or two of her pipe. All the while she looked at Hicks. 'You can't be a detective inspector,' she announced confidently. 'You're too fat.' She jabbed the stem of her pipe into Hick's coat and retreated back to her father.

Hicks noticed those around him smirk and resume their conversations. Perhaps they thought it all part of Springer's game. Whatever game that was. The inspector turned to the sergeant by his side, his eyebrows raised in expectation of an explanation.

'My apologies,' Springer smiled. 'But I thought I'd try a different tack. That man Cooper is hiding something.'

'That might well be,' Hicks seethed. 'But I do not think exposing me to ridicule will have helped in my investigation.'

'The two cases are not linked,' replied Springer, innocently. 'The one will not affect the other.'

Hicks rose unsteadily to his feet. 'Where is this 'City Barge'?'

he demanded.

Sergeant Springer pointed to a low building set some feet back from the water's edge, a sign outside swinging in the gentle breeze.

The upstairs bar at The City Barge was snug, to say the least. Hicks was forced to both remove his hat and duck his head to avoid the low beams in the ceiling. A fireplace, empty of fuel at this time of year, dominated the far wall opposite a long bar. The sergeant led Hicks through the crush of drinkers and diners to a small, recently vacated table by the window. Hicks noticed the sawdust on the floor wasn't perhaps as clean as it might have been. The pumps on the bar were tarnished with rust. It seemed just his sort of place.

The inspector eased himself gratefully into his seat and leaned forward to look down to the strand. There he saw the rough-looking man Springer had conversed with. Cooper. He was marching his daughter away to a rowing boat, his fingers pinching at her ear.

'They grow osiers on the island,' offered Springer as he sat. He snapped his fingers at a young man behind the bar. 'His daughter weaves the sticks into baskets for sale along the river.' Nodding to the barman, he held up two fingers and mimed shovelling food into his mouth. The barman gestured in understanding and set about preparing food and drink for the two policemen.

'How do they live?' It seemed a world apart from the rarefied surroundings in which Hicks had spent his morning.

'Like everyone else along here. There is employment to be found in the boathouses, malthouses and conservancy works but it is not well paid and workers are ten a penny. Cooper has got it right and found a nice little market for himself.' Springer leaned back as the young barman delivered two pewter tankards of foaming ale to the table. He noticed Hicks' eyes light up in appreciation.

'But how does he find work as a smithy on an island?' the portly inspector asked between sips.

'Easily enough,' replied Springer, a moustache of beery foam upon his upper lip. 'He takes commissions on the shore here most mornings as his daughter rows the river with her baskets. He fashions tools.'

Hicks nodded appreciatively as a cold collation was placed before him. Slices of cooked and cured meats were arranged upon a hunk of bread. A limp sprig of celery served for a garnish. Just as he was about to take his first bite, however, he was interrupted by a shout from the bar.

'How did you find the Metternichs?'

Hicks turned with a slice of smoked ham halfway to his lips. Lurching towards him with all the enthusiasm of an eager puppy, was a loud man in an even louder suit, a purple cravat tied at his throat. Hicks' face fell as the man drew another chair up to the table.

'It's quite the Aladdin's Cave, ain't it?' Geraint Fernsby leaned his elbows upon the table. Even among the natural aromas of the bar, Hicks could smell the beer upon his breath. He had clearly been drinking for some time.

'You are no doubt wondering at my presence here at such an hour.' Fernsby slurred his words as he spoke. 'It is because this is where I find all the best stories for The Herald.' He tapped the side of his nose with a finger. Hicks noticed he took a while to find it. 'You'd be surprised just how lubricating a pint or two can be.' Fernsby smiled broadly at Sergeant Springer who was nodding enthusiastically.

Hicks chewed on his ham, thoughtfully. 'Sergeant Springer

tells me you are not held in high regard at Devonhurst.'

'You could say that.' Fernsby raised his glass in a toast.

'Why would that be?' Hicks pulled a string of gristle from his mouth.

'Because I'm on to him!' Fernsby announced in triumph.

'Oh? How so?'

Springer's eyes were alive with mischief. He picked up Fernsby's tale as the newspaperman took a draft of his beer. 'It is rumoured that Metternich's wealth has been accrued at the expense of others.' He winked.

'I ran an exposé on him in the Herald a few years back.' Fernsby was clearly proud of himself. 'When he first moved to Chiswick from Prussia.'

'Why?' Hicks was brushing bread crumbs from his beard.

Fernsby leaned back, spreading his hands wide. 'When a wealthy stranger moves into one of the biggest houses in the district, it's only right that we should know just who he is.'

Hicks harrumphed. Fernsby was typical of a new class of man who was not only interested in everybody's business, but felt compelled to tell the world of it. He and people like him were the reason the newspapers were full of the more sensationalist stories that Hicks couldn't abide and that, presumably, accounted for the increase in their sales. It was a truism, Hicks mused without a hint of irony, that people love to gossip.

'What do you know of the Prussian economy?'

To say Hicks was surprised by the question would be an understatement. 'I know all I need to know,' he said cryptically.

Fernsby shared a smile with Springer. The fellow clearly knew nothing, the look said. 'The Prussian Empire had the world at its feet,' Fernsby began. 'It surpassed our own in steel manufacture and railways. The boom began twenty years ago and there were plenty of banks set up to take advantage. Led by a new confidence following unification, the people invested in stock, sometimes heavily. And then, as with all good booms, the bottom fell out.' Fernsby paused in his diatribe to down the rest of his beer. Wiping his lips on his sleeve, he concluded. 'For six years in the seventies, the economy declined. The prices for industrial goods fell and investors were left short. They lost everything. And the banks went in hard.'

Sergeant Springer leapt in. 'And hardest of all, was Die Gründerkasse. One in every five of the corporations it supported was declared bankrupt. The bank recovered what it could from the companies to save its own skin. Even down to the personal effects of the directors.'

'Hence the treasures you saw today in Devonhurst,' Fernsby concluded. 'Did you notice the pictures in the entrance hall?'

Hicks nodded. 'I did.'

'And the sculptures in the parlour?'

'Indeed.'

Fernsby leaned forward again. 'Ill-gotten gains.' He formed the words with relish.

'So Metternich was connected with this Gründerkasse bank?' Hicks was careful to follow the train of thought.

'He was its president!' Fernsby's face was turning a shade of red in his enthusiasm. He had been right, Hicks noted, when he had said that beer was a lubricant. 'I could not make the rumours of embezzlement stick, but it is clear he acted with scant regard for his customers. In fact, he benefited from their misfortune.'

'Is that what you reported in The Chiswick Herald?' the inspector asked.

Fernsby nodded furiously. 'It was.'

'And since we work closely in cooperation with The Herald in our investigations,' Springer explained, 'Mr Metternich is reticent to avail himself of the local police and their services.'

Their story told, the two men sat back, satisfied. As Hicks gazed out to the river, he cast his mind back to the morning spent at Devonhurst. He could not believe any of the staff responsible for the theft, but had they colluded with the thief? Doubtful, he concluded as he lifted his tankard. The thief gained entry with no help. There had been no doors left unlocked, no windows left ajar. All he needed was the knowledge he had to himself. The knowledge of the hidden tunnel.

'How long have the Metternichs lived at Devonhurst?'

'Some five years,' Springer replied.

Hicks was grasping towards something. 'And all the staff were hired by them? They kept none from the previous household?'

Fernsby thought. 'The previous cook and footman were man and wife. They moved with the owners to Scotland. They had two maids who died of the typhoid.' Hicks raised his eyebrows. 'It all made for very good copy,' Fernsby leered.

Hicks thought carefully. 'Sergeant Springer, as we examined the entrance to the tunnel, you mentioned the groundskeeper.'

Springer nodded. 'Yes, Mr Knightly is part time only.'

Hicks shook his great head. Flecks of dried skin fell from his scalp to his shoulders. 'I mean the previous gardener whom you said had been retired.'

'Ah yes,' confirmed Springer, cheerfully. 'That's right.'

'Is he still alive?'

'That I do not know, Inspector Hicks.'

'Mr Fernsby, you made no mention of him.'

Fernsby puffed out his cheeks. 'He was of no interest,' he said simply. 'My articles concentrated on the household. As I understood it, the gardener was not resident at Devonhurst but lived elsewhere.'

Hicks dropped his empty tankard to the table with a clang. 'Do you have a name for him, Springer? It might be useful to find the man. He might have knowledge of the tunnel.'

Sergeant Springer pulled his notebook from his pocket. 'I am sure one of the staff mentioned his name during my investigations.' He leafed through the pages until he found his place. 'Aha!' he exclaimed with a note of triumph. 'Here we are, inspector. His name was Barraclough.'

Detective Inspector Hicks was blowed if he was going to walk back to the High Road. Soon, he was rattling through the streets of Chiswick in the back of a smart brougham he had requisitioned at Chiswick Junction station. The journey took him past new houses, each identical to the other, and older houses of more individual designs. For his money, the latest generation of architects were determined to homogenise the country with their creations. Soon, mused Hicks as he sped through Blenheim Road, every town would look much like another. As Wellesley Road joined with Turnham Green, the driver steered his charges into a hard left turn onto Arlington Park Gardens. Here, the houses were grander. To his right, Hicks saw a row of elegant four-storey townhouses painted in jaunty colours. Turning his attention to the pavement, he saw Herbert Roundtree the paperboy standing outside a public house on the High Road. Rapping on the roof with his knuckles to tell the driver he should stop, Hicks pushed open the door and stepped onto the road.

The inspector noticed the young lad's face fall as he saw him.

'Oh, no.' Bert rolled his eyes. 'Not you again. Come to box me ears, 'ave you?'

Hicks held his hands up in a gesture of capitulation. 'I have come to ask your help.'

''Elp?' the boy screamed. 'After 'ow you treated me this morning? I don't owe you nuffin'.'

'You mentioned a man I had met on the tram this morning.'

The boy's eyes narrowed. He sensed he was at an advantage.

'Might have,' he said slyly.

It was Hicks' turn to roll his eyes. Reaching into his pocket, he pulled out a fistful of loose change. The lad looked it over, clearly deciding if it might be enough. Satisfied that it was, he took the coins from Hicks' open palm and dropped them into a leather pouch at his side.

'Barraclough, his name is.'

'Do you know the man?' Hicks was trying to adopt a tone of appeasement.

'Like I said this mornin', I never miss a trick.' Bert tugged at his earlobe. 'I keep these open. And these an' all.' He pointed to his eyes.

'Well done.' Hicks attempted a smile. In truth the boy was trying his patience. 'So, you know him?'

'Better than he knows himself,' the lad beamed. 'He barely knows who he is most o'the time.'

Hicks sighed. 'You mentioned he rides the tram all day. Is that right?'

'What is it o'clock?' the boy asked, suddenly.

Hicks snapped his fob watch open to peer at the dial. 'Almost a quarter to three.'

'Then he'll be along at half past the hour. There's the stop.' Herbert Roundtree pointed across the busy road to where a sign stood, propped up against a tobacconist's kiosk.

'You said he spent his nights at The Duke Of Sussex public house.' Hicks had heard much of the altercation there on the night of the robbery.

'Did I?' The paperboy blinked innocently, holding his empty palm out in front of him.

Hicks sighed and patted his pockets. He was about to protest that he had no change when the boy leaned forward.

'Tobacco will do,' he smiled.

It was all Hicks could do to refrain from pinching his ears.

Instead, he pulled his tobacco pouch from his coat pocket. Deliberately filling the bowl of his own pipe first, he then took a pinch and held it out to the boy. Bert had taken out a small clay pipe of his own, the bowl fashioned into the shape of an elephant's head. With a look, he gave the inspector to understand that more would be needed. Hicks relented and gave the lad enough to fill the hole in the elephant's head.

'The Duke Of Sussex is but a quarter of a mile behind you, over the railway and turn right. You could make it there and back in good time for the tram, I reckon.' He looked the inspector up and down. 'Even a big bloke like you.'

Glad to have the information he needed, Hicks turned to follow the directions he had been given.

'Hey!' the boy called after him. He had been sorting through his change. 'This 'ere money's foreign!'

Inspector Hicks followed the loop of the road around to the north of the High Road. He crossed the railway tracks at Chiswick Park station and passed under the bridge, from where he could see The Duke Of Sussex standing on a corner near Acton Common. Its large windows gave Hicks the perfect opportunity to peer inside. Much like The City Barge, it was full of patrons even at this hour. The inspector could clearly see the landlord at his bar, manhandling a barrel of beer into the cellar. A smaller window by the door was dangerously cracked, perhaps as a result of the affray Hicks had heard so much about. Two planks of wood had been nailed across its width to prevent it falling out completely. Hicks pushed at the door. The bar, which had been humming with conversation and noise, was suddenly silent. Glasses and tankards were held in transit to lips. All eyes were upon him. The man nearest to him, a small agricultural worker in a dusty smock, spat on the floor near his feet and challenged him with a look to respond. Hicks swallowed and swaggered to the bar, eager to face out whatever threat was implied by the silence. The clientele here was of a rougher sort than at The City Barge. Many of them were drunk already. The air was heavy with menace.

'Lost, ain't ya?' A man at the bar swayed dangerously close to the inspector.

Hicks looked around him. 'Not at all.' He held the man's gaze, pulling himself up to his full, intimidating height. 'Just out for a walk on this fine September day.'

'Then, I think you'd better continue with your little walk.' The man's voice was like ground glass. He had a chin full of stubble and deep-set eyes. His hair was wild and unruly.

'I could do that,' agreed Hicks. 'Or I could buy you a drink for your pains.'

'Got money, 'ave ya?'

'Not as much as I had but a few minutes ago,' answered Hicks truthfully, his mind on the change he had given to Herbert Roundtree. There had been a sixpence in amongst the foreign change. 'But enough for two pints of the landlord's finest.'

The rough man looked deep into Hicks' eyes in a silent challenge, then clapped him on the shoulder as if they were the oldest of friends.

'Then, that's good enough for me!' he exclaimed.

Hicks watched as the landlord pulled at the pumps on his bar and delivered two jars of foam. Hicks' companion took his with a wink and a tip of his head. As he sauntered away unsteadily to join some men at the window, those in the saloon took it as a cue to continue with their conversations.

Hicks turned to the landlord. He was a large man with a muscular frame and chiselled jaw.

'I am looking for a man,' Hicks began. 'A friend. I believe he lives Chiswick way.'

The landlord looked the inspector up and down and laughed.

'I doubt if you're a friend of any who drinks in here.'

'His name is Barraclough,' Hicks whispered so as not to be overheard. 'I hear he's fallen on hard times.'

Seemingly alarmed at the mention of Barraclough's name, the landlord looked around him and leaned forward on his elbows. 'Finish your beer and meet me in the yard on Beaconsfield Road, just behind us.' He lowered his voice even more. 'And be sure not to mention that name again while you're in this bar.'

With that, the landlord bent to lift an empty barrel to his shoulder. Jamming a smoking cheroot between his lips, he made his way through an open door to the yard outside. Hicks lit his pipe and drew deeply, the fumes rising to mingle with the fog in the bar. Leaning as nonchalantly as he could against the corner of the counter, he downed his pint and wiped the foam from his lips with the back of his hand.

'You're welcome any time,' chimed the man by the window, raising his glass to the inspector with a cackle. 'Enjoy the rest of your walk.' He gave a ghastly wink as he downed the dregs of his beer, then turned to join his companions once more. Hicks ambled from the pub with a nod of his head to those that cared to watch him leave, then made his way round the corner. He caught sight of St Alban's church behind the trees on Acton Common. It was a symbol, thought Hicks, of the eternal optimism of the Christian Church; that a man might exit an establishment such as The Duke Of Sussex and feel the need to commune with God.

The inspector was presented with a rickety gate in the wall. Beyond it, he could hear the clatter of bottles and crates. Pushing against the gate, he found himself in The Duke Of Sussex's yard. The rich aroma of swilled beer rose to his nostrils. It had a sweet and heady fragrance. Looking around him, he saw piles of crates that were full of bottles of green and brown glass. Wooden barrels were stacked against a far wall.

Further along the inside wall, he could see more bottles, empty this time, laying in great skips for collection. The floor was wet and sticky with wasted beer. In a corner, Hicks saw the landlord. He was leaning idly against the wall, his cheroot hanging from his lips.

'What do you know of Barraclough?' the landlord asked.

Hicks cleared his throat as he walked into the yard. 'I know he has found himself in a bit of trouble these last few years.'

'That he has,' the landlord replied. 'Enough trouble to see him sacked from Devonhurst. You know he was the gardener for the Cavendish family? The new owners gave him the heave-ho quick enough.'

Hicks nodded. In actual fact, this was the first time he had heard the name of the house's previous occupants. 'Was it the drink?' Hicks thought fast. 'It was a terrible problem when last I saw him.'

'It's always the drink.' The landlord said, sadly. 'When you see him, tell him I'll be needing payment for that window.'

'What happened?' Hicks asked, as innocently as he could.

'He was lucky to walk out my pub on his two legs, I'll tell you that.'

'I have heard he has been causing trouble.' Hicks was treading carefully.

'He's always causing trouble,' the landlord hissed. 'In fact, he courts it.'

'How so?'

'Barraclough flies closer to the wind than most of us. He's a poacher and a hustler. Been in trouble with the law a few times.' Hicks shifted his weight, uncomfortably. 'I've had the bluebottles from the police station all over my pub these last couple of days on account of what happened here on Saturday.' The landlord leaned in. 'I can't afford to have the police snooping round here,' he confided.

Hicks looked around the yard with fresh eyes. Just how much of the landlord's trade was legal he couldn't tell. Yet he could guess that at least some of this alcohol was acquired illicitly. The inspector had to concede it was the only way many publicans could make a living. Regulation and law was so strict with regard to licensing, that any loophole was seized upon.

'Tell me about Saturday night,' Hicks said, turning his attention back to the brawny man beside him.

'Barraclough was in here late. He didn't appear until after I'd rung the bell.' The landlord's eyes twinkled. 'I had a lock-in until the small hours. Just don't tell the Peelers.' He nudged Hicks in the ribs. The inspector sneered back. 'He'd done a job for someone that night. I dunno what it was. Poaching maybe.'

Hicks was making mental notes as the landlord spoke, desperately trying to match this new information with that which had come before.

'Anyhow,' the landlord continued, 'he clearly wasn't happy with his payment. I saw it all from the bar. Trouble is round here, if there's any trouble, others are like to join in. Soon enough, it was a brawl and he ended up fair near throwing the man through my window.'

'Which man would that be?' Hicks opened his eyes wide in expectation.

'The smith from Oli's Island,' the landlord said. 'Cooper, his name is.'

'Cooper? Yeah, I know 'im.' Herbert Roundtree was sitting on a low wall, a hot pie in his hands courtesy of the detective inspector beside him. Hicks had his hands deep in his pockets. His brow was furrowed in thought.

'What can you tell me of him?' Hicks sat next to him. He hadn't walked so far in months. His shoes were pinching at his feet and he was sure he had a blister.

'He's rough,' Bert said simply as he bit into his crust. 'Always causing trouble. He gets up to all sorts on that island of his.'

'All sorts?' Hicks' eyebrows rose beneath the brim of his hat.

'Yeah, counterfeitin' stuff. Makin' things and passin' 'em off as valuable.' The lad licked the grease from his lips. 'Some people will fall for anyfing.'

Hicks nodded. That much was true. The inspector had never ceased to be amazed just how much the gullible public would swallow. Particularly if they were told something they wanted to believe.

'Even his name ain't real.'

'Really?'

'Nah, foreign, ain't he? He changed it to Cooper when he arrived in England.'

'How do you know all this?' Hicks looked at his young companion with a new respect.

'I keep my eyes and ears open, detective inspector,' Bert explained. 'Besides, I'm sweet on his young girl, Lucy.' Hicks thought he saw a blush rise beneath the grime on the boy's cheeks. 'I sometimes 'elp her sell her baskets on the river.' He noticed Hicks' look. 'We get to talking, that's all.'

'So, what was his family's previous name?' Hicks leaned his hands upon his knees in anticipation.

'Küfer, or somethin',' Bert said, breezily. 'Cooper was the nearest they could get in our lingo.'

Hicks thought back to his encounter with Cooper on the banks of The Thames. The man had given no indication that he was anything but English born and bred.

'Do you know how long Cooper has been in England?' Hicks asked.

'Maybe fifteen years. Came 'ere to make a fresh start, Lucy

says.'

'And where is he from?'

'With a name like Küfer, I would have thought it obvious.' Bert finished off the last of his pie. 'Germany o'course!'

Just as Hicks let that sink in, his attention was drawn to the rattle of a tram arriving at the stop across the street.

'Bert,' he said, suddenly insistent, 'I want you to run to Chiswick Police Station as fast as you can. Tell Sergeant Springer to meet me at The City Barge in thirty minutes.' Hicks rose to his feet with more purpose than Bert had seen in him all day.

'Where you goin'?' the lad asked as he sprang from the wall.

Hicks was already halfway across the road, his coat tails flapping behind him. 'To show Sergeant Springer,' he called back, 'that all the book-learnin' in the world is no substitute for the instinct of a good detective.'

The Thames was still busy, although the labourers that had earlier thronged along its bank had returned to their work in the boat sheds, factories and workshops along the strand.

Barraclough had come easily enough. Already in his cups, he had been napping on the tram as was his wont. Hicks had dragged him from the vehicle with little resistance and managed to hail a cab with one hand whilst holding Barraclough by the lapels in the other.

Soon, they were clattering towards the river.

Barraclough flopped against the side of the hansom, barely conscious, a half-empty bottle of gin nestled in his lap. Hicks was amused to see him stroke it occasionally as one might stroke a pet. His black eye was even more prominent in the late afternoon light.

'What did he offer you, Barraclough?' Hicks breathed.

'Who? For what?' Barraclough's words were slurred. A string

of drool fell from his lower lip as he spoke.

'Cooper,' Hicks replied. 'What did he offer you?'

'Cooper!' the man suddenly exclaimed. 'Don't talk to me about Cooper! Never trust a foreigner, my old man would say. He was right.' He swung a fist dangerously before him as he spat out his words. It was as if he imagined Cooper right in front of him. 'I should never have told him about that bloomin' tunnel.'

'So he's not to be trusted?' Hicks was leading him on.

'He used me, good and proper. We got to talking and I mentioned a cup I'd seen at Devonhurst. Before I was sacked. Cooper promised me a good price. I should have known he ain't got a penny more than I have.'

'Promised you for a good price for what, Barraclough?' Hicks steadied himself against the roll of the carriage as they neared the Thames. If he could get a confession from Barraclough it would go easier for him back at The Yard. If not, he could always say he had. Barraclough was nodding off to the motion of the wheels on the cobbles. As the carriage slowed, Hicks reached over to shake the drunk by the lapels. 'A good price for what?'

'The cup!' Barraclough drooled. 'The Traubenkopal.'

With that, he sunk back into his seat and into a deep, snoring slumber. Hicks opened the wooden flaps at his lap to alight from the carriage, only to see Sergeant Springer was already waiting for him.

'I cannot condone your methods, Detective Inspector Hicks,' he said. 'But I heard that confession well enough.' Springer turned to a young constable behind him. 'Turner, get this man to the station.'

'We need a boat,' wheezed Hicks as he lumbered towards the sergeant. 'We have to get to Cooper on the island.' He looked across to see Cooper's boat tied to the jetty half way across the river. His daughter sat with the fishing rod in her hands.

Springer turned to indicate the riverbank beneath him. There were any number of craft, all tied to their moorings. 'Take your pick, Inspector Hicks,' he said with a smile.

The tide was on the turn and Springer had to fight to keep a straight course. The two men had requisitioned a small skiff from the riverbank, Springer choosing its narrow bows and sharp prow to give him the extra speed he felt he might need. Hicks, of course, was happy to let Springer take the strain. Rowing towards Kew Bridge at first, the sergeant turned at the last moment to let the current carry them to the island, keeping close to the shore on the Kew side of the river. Hicks could see the smoke rising from Cooper's smithy and was sure he could even hear the clang of hammer on metal. It was as well, thought the inspector, that the man was busy at his work. The noise of his tools might well disguise their approach.

Soon, they were drawing close to the south side of the island. To his right, Hicks could see Kew docks and the cottages that had been built to house the workers. Cranes lifted coal from the deck of a berthed barge. The bustle of the river traffic in and around the dock served to give their little craft good cover. Ahead of him, the inspector saw a small, muddy beach on the island. He pointed over Springer's back to alert him. Looking behind him, the police sergeant nodded his assent and leaned harder into the oars. In just a few moments, Hicks felt the bottom of the boat scrape against the mud.

'It's as close as we'll get,' rasped Springer as he secured his oars. 'Follow me.'

The boat beached firmly on the muddy shore, Springer loped off into the scrubby patches of willow that sprung up from the island. Keeping low, he skirted around the shore heading towards the source of the smoke; Cooper's smithy. It took a while for Hicks to free himself of the boat. With Springer disappearing out of sight, he feared he might never get out. His wide hips were jammed between both sides of the skiff's narrow hull. It took a mighty effort to ease himself free. At last, he staggered to the bank, his boots sinking in the stinking mud beneath him. Swiping at the willow saplings with his hands, he made his way towards the smoke.

Springer had made quick progress with his youthful gait. As he cleared the osiers, he found himself approaching a small clearing. In the middle of it stood a small brick building that seemed part cottage and part workshop. The noise of the hammer beat out its metallic rhythm. He slowed his step as he approached, careful to stay low against the scrubby foliage that sprouted around him. Glancing round for Inspector Hicks, Springer saw that he was alone. Reasoning that Hicks would be with him shortly, the sergeant crouched to wait, only to find himself face to face with a young girl in a ragged smock and straw hat. Holding a fishing rod in one hand and a pair of perch in the other, Lucy Cooper opened her eyes wide in surprise and gave a long, loud scream.

Hicks stopped in his tracks. The scream pierced the air. It sounded as if it was close. Reasoning it spelled only bad news for Sergeant Springer, Hicks thought fast. His best hope, he reasoned, was to skirt around the edge of the island and approach the smithy from behind, in the hope that Cooper would not notice. Lifting his coat from his ankles, he stepped carefully along the foreshore. Soon he could hear voices.

'Come away, Lucy. It's all right, girl.'

So, thought Hicks, the young girl had clearly stumbled across Springer in his progress to the smithy.

'Just what do you want, filth?' Hicks could hear Cooper

snarling.

'Don't do anything rash, Cooper,' Hicks heard Springer respond. 'Keep a cool head and you'll only go down for robbery. Think of the girl.'

'Robbery be blowed,' the smith snapped back. 'How can you steal what's yours in the first place?'

Hicks could see the small brick building now. Keeping it to his left, he picked his way carefully through the detritus that surrounded it. Discarded hunks, strips and sheets of metal littered the ground. Half empty vats of noxious chemicals threatened to block his path. The spoils of the counterfeiter. Sergeant Springer was wrong. Cooper would be facing more than a charge of robbery. The smithy was a peculiar construction. Side rooms sprang from the main building in a haphazard fashion, often little more than brick hovels. Peering through the scrub, he saw the main area of the house was given over to a workshop. A forge glowed a fierce red at its heart, but he could see shelves laden with tools. Boxes were scattered about the place. One or two were on their side, spilling their contents of fake and glass jewellery onto the mud.

'How was the Traubenpokal yours, Cooper? Mr Metternich brought it with him from Germany.'

'Taken from my father!' Cooper snarled. 'Metternich was happy enough to have my father's money as long as it made him interest. But the moment the market crashed, he demanded repayment of his loans.'

Hicks had circled the smithy completely and found himself behind Cooper. Keeping flat against the wall of the building, he could see his daughter, Lucy, had run to his side. Cooper was waving his smith's tongs before him as he spoke. The tips glowed white.

'When my father couldn't pay, he was repossessed. The bank stripped him of his assets. Everything he had worked for in his life went to Noah Metternich.'

'Including the Traubenpokal?' Hicks could see Springer standing stock-still, fearful of just what Cooper might do with those tongs.

'It's a thing of beauty, Sergeant Springer. The most valuable thing in my father's possession. Its loss was a terrible blow.' He was clutching his daughter to his side. From the crack in his voice as he spoke, Hicks could tell the man was crying. 'It was too much for him. My father took his own life almost twenty years ago. That's when I moved to England to start a new life.' Hicks saw Cooper spread his arms. 'Some life,' he sneered.

'You can tell all this to the judge, Cooper.' Springer had sight of Hicks now and was determined to keep the smith's attention. 'Barraclough has already admitted his part.'

'You'd take the word of a drunk?'

'I don't think even a drunkard would confect such a story. It is a tale full of profound sadness and terrible coincidence.'

'The only coincidence was a happy one, Sergeant Springer,' Cooper was insisting. 'That Noah Metternich and his wife moved to a house a stone's throw away from where I had made my home. How helpful of The Herald to print the details!'

By now, Hicks had shrugged off his coat. If he and Springer were to make any progress, Cooper must be disarmed of his tongs. Holding his coat before him, the inspector advanced slowly towards the smith from behind. Judging the distance as best he could, Hicks paused and took a breath.

'Herr Küfer!' he cried. In that very moment, he charged at Cooper. The smith turned instinctively to the source of the cry, to see the portly inspector barrelling towards him. Before he could even raise his hands in self-defence, Hicks threw his coat at the man. Cooper became tangled in the voluminous sleeves and lapels of Hicks great coat and let out a cry. Lucy screamed as Springer lunged towards her.

'It's all right, my girl,' he soothed as Cooper thrashed about. He let the tongs fall in his efforts to free himself. Hicks took that as a cue to launch himself at the smith. His great bulk came crashing down upon the unfortunate man. In no time at all, Cooper was pinned to the ground, his legs and arms becoming even more tangled in Hicks' coat as they flailed around.

'I've got him, Springer!' Hicks called as he rolled on the ground. The inspector squeezed hard at the writhing form beneath him and, eventually, he was still. He could feel Cooper breathing through the coat. Every now and then an expletive would rise from the material, aimed squarely at the two policemen who had been the smith's downfall.

Springer bent to the ground and reached for a pocket in his tunic. Finding the man's hands beneath the folds of Hicks' coat, he snapped on a pair of cuffs and hauled Cooper to his feet. Lucy was subdued now and ran to her father's side, hugging at his legs for comfort.

The criminal secured, Springer turned to see Hicks lumbering into the tumbledown smithy. He was looking around the forge in the centre of the large, open workshop. The sergeant could see he was breathing heavily after his tussle with Cooper, clutching at his chest to settle its rise and fall. Peering into the mouth of the forge, Hicks noticed a quantity of molten metal in a dish suspended above the white-hot coals.

'Hicks!' called Springer. 'What is it? Are we too late?'

Suddenly, Hicks stepped over a large pair of bellows to reach for an object on a shelf. It was wrapped in an old oily rag, but Hicks fancied he had seen the glint of gold beneath. As he let the rag fall to the ground, he was presented with as beautiful an object as he had ever seen. The Traubenpokal was bigger than he'd imagined from Fernsby's picture, standing a good two feet tall. From a sturdy plinth, it rose via a slender stem in the form of some ancient god or sprite - Bacchus, perhaps - to a bowl fashioned from a bunch of grapes. The whole thing shone in the evening sun, despite the tarnish it had accrued over the past two days in Cooper's workshop.

'No Springer, we're not too late.' He gave the sergeant a look of triumph. 'Not too late, at all.'

Springer's face broke into a wide smile. Hooking Cooper's arms up behind his back, he turned to march the man and his daughter to the boat. He paused beneath a low branch and turned back to Hicks. 'I shall be sure you are the subject of a favourable profile in the Chiswick Herald!'

The bluff inspector couldn't suppress his smile. As he clamped the bit of his pipe between his teeth, he mused just how splendid the article would look upon the wall of his new office, in the place of that old map.

The next two short stories take place following the events of the fourth novel in the Bowman Of The Yard series, THE PHANTOM IN THE FOG.

RICHARD JAMES

THE STEPNEY BLACKMAILING

NOVEMBER, 1892

In the week since his return to Scotland Yard, Detective Inspector George Bowman had yet to be presented with a case. He had spent his time, instead, in countless meetings with the commissioner in an effort to persuade him of his fitness to resume his duties as a detective. With Detective Superintendent Callaghan's reputation in tatters, there had been a re-evaluation at the Yard which had served to profit the beleaguered inspector. His investigations at St Saviour's Dock had been reappraised in the light of Callaghan's recent fall from grace, and Bowman had been the beneficiary of the commissioner's willingness to look again at his part in the case.

"It seems we owe you an apology," Commissioner Bradford announced, his remaining hand twitching in the small of his back as he stood at the window.

"Not at all, sir," Bowman responded, magnanimously.

"I have read Wilkes' report from Colney Hatch," Bradford continued as he turned into the room. "He has the utmost confidence in your recovery."

"As do I," Bowman asserted, meeting the commissioner's unfaltering gaze with a degree of confidence he had not felt for some time.

Commissioner Bradford sighed. "In truth, George, I need you back." He motioned that Bowman should join him at his desk, and the detective inspector slid out a chair.

Bradford ran a hand over his luxuriant moustaches. It was clear he was choosing his words with care. "Superintendent Callaghan's activities have placed a certain pall over the Yard," he began, quietly. "It is a scandal from which we may never recover."

Bowman nodded. He had little doubt the commissioner had

seen the headlines in the newspapers. All week they had screamed of failings at the Yard and the concealment of a killer within its very walls. There had been calls for greater scrutiny of the detectives in its employ. The commissioner had had to answer to the Prime Minister himself as well as issuing an apology to the citizens of London via the Home Secretary. It had left him and the detectives of Scotland Yard diminished.

"I dare not show you the letters I have received from the public," Bradford huffed.

The Evening Standard had instigated a letter writing campaign, encouraging members of the public to make their feelings known to those who were, after all, their servants.

"We must be ever more tenacious in our pursuit of crime," Bowman offered, thoughtfully. "It is the only way to regain their trust."

Bradford narrowed his eyes at the remark. "Which is why I need to be assured of your recovery."

Bowman met the commissioner's gaze again. "I can give you my word, sir," he said, a note of steel in his voice.

Commissioner Bradford seemed satisfied at the response. He leaned his elbow on the desk. "Inspector Hicks will be missed, of course."

Bowman nodded. "He will, sir. He was an asset to The Force." The remark hung in the air for a moment as Bradford gathered his thoughts.

"We are under scrutiny as never before." The commissioner leaned in. "I cannot afford another mis-step."

"I understand, sir."

"Then that'll be all, Inspector Bowman." With that, the commissioner rose from his seat and returned to glower out the window into the November gloom.

Bowman paused as he reached for the door. "Commissioner Bradford," he said as he turned back to the simmering figure by the window. "I would like to recommend Detective Sergeant Graves for advancement. His conduct, both professional and personal, has never been anything short of exemplary. If you are looking for detective inspectors who can command the trust of the press and public alike, I can think of no man more worthy of the rank." Bowman's moustache twitched as he awaited a response.

Bradford cocked his head as he thought the matter over. "I shall consider it," he said, at last.

Bowman was satisfied he had pleaded Graves' case adroitly enough. With a murmur of thanks, he opened the door and left the commissioner to his ruminations.

The journey to Stepney was taken in silence. Detective Inspector Bowman gazed mournfully from the cab window as it sped through the drab November streets. His black coat and hat served only to accentuate his sombre expression, but Sergeant Graves was pleased to note a certain vitality in the inspector that he had not seen for several months.

He had spent the morning helping Bowman to rearrange his office. The map had been returned to its usual place upon the wall above the bureau, though Bowman had made a point of finding a new place for Hicks' framed newspaper account of his investigations into the robbery at Chiswick. The portly inspector's ephemera that Bowman had found littered about the place, had been boxed to be returned to his sister. She was the only surviving member of Hicks' family that he knew of, and it felt only right that their ownership should fall to her. Graves had suggested they take it with them to the funeral.

Everything in its place once more, the young sergeant had wrapped a black tie around his wing-collared shirt and shrugged on a charcoal frock coat.

Their cab took them past many sites of previous

investigations, particularly those at St Katharine Docks. If Bowman felt anything at all as the site of the bomb in the East Basin flashed past he did not show it. Nor did he so much as blink at the near-completed Tower Bridge, in whose shadow he had found himself in thrall to Callaghan's machinations. For all that he was silent, however, Graves was pleased to see that Bowman had shrugged off the pall of melancholy which had, of late, been wont to settle about him. Ever the optimist, he dared to believe for a moment that Inspector Bowman's recent stay at Colney Hatch might just have cured him of his melancholy. For all that Bowman's demeanour seemed markedly different, Graves couldn't help but find himself on tenterhooks, looking for any sign of Bowman's manic episodes. As if in response to the young sergeant's unspoken thoughts, Bowman turned to face his companion as they rattled away from the River Thames to offer him a rueful smile.

St Dunstan's Church had been a place of worship for almost a thousand years. During the arrival of the Huguenots in the seventeenth century, the Irish in the eighteenth and now the Jewish Ashkenazi refugees from the continent, it had stood sentinel in the heart of the community. Its square tower seemed a reminder of the solidity of faith.

As he stepped from the cab footplate by the church gate, Bowman took a moment to take in the scene. With the light of the sun smeared across the grey sky and the russet leaves collecting in drifts by the church, it reminded him of nothing less than an artist's palette. His eye fell upon the few stragglers who were braving the weather. Sections of the graveyard had been given over to public gardens and, even on this greyest of days, Bowman could see that several passers by had paused to sit in the gloom. A young man held his head in his hands before rising to walk through the gate to the High Street, tipping his hat to a young woman with a basket. She had two young children in tow, one of whom was kicking his way through the beech leaves on the pavement as he walked. A couple leaned against a tree near the church wall in earnest conversation. The man wrung his hat in his hands anxiously while his companion looked demurely up at him from beneath the brim of her bonnet. Limping past them both, an old soldier puffed out his cheeks against the cold, a brace of medals swinging from his chest. Lastly, Bowman noticed a lone woman with steel grey hair and ruddy cheeks sitting on a bench beneath a larch tree. She periodically flicked her eyes to the churchyard entrance and Bowman guessed she must be waiting for something or someone. Each one of these people, the inspector knew, would have a story to tell, and not all of them would be happy.

'There's our bolt hole,' said Graves cheerfully, waving at the building by the roadside. Bowman looked round to see a public house nestled in the corner of Stepney High Street and Spring Garden Place. Glancing at his companion, he noticed Graves look away, suddenly sheepish.

'It's all right, Sergeant Graves,' Bowman soothed. 'I'd be happy to join you for a swift one after the funeral. It seems appropriate, somehow.' Graves was surprised to see him flash a smile before turning towards the church gates. 'There they are,' the inspector breathed.

The two men stepped back from the pavement as a horse drawn hearse pulled up to the church gate, preceded by a smaller, sombre carriage. A small crowd gathered as the pallbearers disembarked and slowly slid a coffin from the back of the carriage behind them. They each gave a lurch as they hoisted it onto their shoulders, a sign that the body within was clearly heavier than they had expected. Linking arms around shoulders, they began their sedate walk through the churchyard towards a mound of earth that had been excavated by a far wall.

As the two men watched, a smart brougham delivered a small shrew of a woman to the kerbside. Bowman recognised her at once. Her features were even more drawn than when they last had met, but it was clearly Florence Habgood, Inspector Hicks' sister. Dressed in black, she hid her face behind a handkerchief as she followed the sparse cortege through the gates to the cemetery beyond. If she noticed the two men standing outside the public house on the corner, she didn't show it. Perhaps her indifference was a legacy of their last meeting. During his investigations at the Hackney Union Workhouse, Bowman had exposed Hicks for protecting his sister against charges of murder, even going so far as to withhold incriminating evidence. Bowman had no doubt Mrs Habgood bore a grudge over her brother's treatment at his hands.

Bowman turned to Graves with a sigh. 'Shall we?' At a nod from his companion, the inspector pulled his collar about his neck and the two detectives followed the diminutive woman through the gates.

They were met at the graveside by the lean figure of the local vicar. He regarded proceedings through a pair of pince-nez balanced delicately at the end of his nose. He already looked bored with proceedings. Noticing Mrs Habgood approaching, the vicar attempted to soften his features but succeeded only in looking more haughty still. Florence Habgood nodded in response and dabbed at her eyes with her lace handkerchief. Bowman settled himself some feet away, his feet planted firmly in the grass, hands behind his back. He heard Graves let out a breath as the coffin approached.

The casket was of a polished walnut with ornate handles. As the pallbearers lowered it onto the planks that straddled the grave, Bowman noticed a gleaming breastplate had been added. 'Ignatius Aloysius Hicks,' it read, '19th October, 1892, aged 42 years'. Bowman could see the curious shapes of reflected branches contorted upon its surface. He could tell it was a costly affair. Casting his eye over Florence's mourning weeds, he doubted Hicks' sister had paid for the funeral. The tears and patches in the fabric spoke of a meagre income. Bowman was in no doubt that the inspector's own estate had been pressed into the service of providing him an appropriate farewell. With no other family that Bowman was aware of, the inspector hazarded that Florence alone would benefit from Hicks' legacy. It would surely be enough to save her from the rigours of life in service at the Hackney Union Warehouse.

It was clear by now that there were to be no other mourners. Clearly disappointed at the low turnout, the vicar pursed his lips. 'Man that is born of a woman hath but a short time to live,' he began in a thin, reedy voice, 'and is full of misery. He cometh up, and is cut down, like a flower; he fleeth as it were a shadow, and never continueth in one stay.'

Bowman noticed Florence Habgood sobbing with abandon and resisted the urge to move to comfort her.

The vicar adjusted his cassock about him, the better to keep out the keen November wind, and continued his reading from the book he held in his gnarled hands.

'In the midst of life,' he intoned, 'we are in death: of whom may we seek for succour, but of thee, O Lord, who for our sins art justly displeased?'

Bowman felt a nudge at his elbow and looked round to see Sergeant Graves. nodding towards the bench beneath the larch. There sat the woman Bowman had spotted from the gate, her keen eyes clearly following proceedings with care.

Bowman's thoughts were interrupted by a movement at the graveside. Florence was bending to pluck a handful of dirt from the ground as the planks were removed from beneath the coffin. Bracing themselves against the weight, the pallbearers let the supporting straps run through their hands and the casket made its descent.

'For as much as it hath pleased Almighty God of his great mercy,' the vicar continued, 'to take unto himself the soul of our dear brother here departed: we therefore commit his body to the ground.' At this, Florence leaned in to throw the dirt upon the coffin. As if it were a signal, Bowman and Graves did the same, bending to scoop the grit from the ground and send it scattering across the coffin lid below. 'Earth to earth, ashes to ashes, dust to dust; in sure and certain hope of the Resurrection to eternal life, through our Lord Jesus Christ; who shall change our vile body, that it may be like unto his glorious body, according to the mighty working, whereby he is able to subdue all things to himself.'

There was a brief silence while Florence seemed to stand in prayer, then the vicar concluded hurriedly with a curt, 'Lord, have mercy upon us.' Bowman noticed him glance surreptitiously back to the church, where a man leaned on a shovel in anticipation of his morning's work.

Turning to Mrs Habgood, the vicar laid a consoling hand upon her shoulder and attempted a look of comfort. The poor woman nodded in response and dabbed at her nose. With a final look around him, the vicar retreated back into the church and, at a signal, the pallbearers made their way from the graveside. Bowman noticed the man with the shovel was gripping at its handle in his impatience.

Clearing his throat, the detective inspector stepped forward, at last. 'Mrs Habgood,' he began, 'may I offer my condolences?'

She deigned to lift her gaze towards him. 'Is this all Scotland Yard could manage?' she spat, indignantly.

Bowman looked back at his companion. Graves was shuffling nervously at the graveside.

'We are here to represent the whole of The Metropolitan

Police Force,' Bowman began with some feeling. 'Your brother's loss will be keenly felt.'

Florence bristled. 'Indeed? Yet not so keenly felt that you should visit the coffin at home.'

Bowman swallowed hard, his neck suddenly burning beneath his collar. 'We did not wish to intrude upon family matters,' he soothed.

Florence nodded, seemingly satisfied with the inspector's response. 'Ignatius spoke of you often, Inspector Bowman, and not always kindly.' Bowman was sure he heard Graves attempting to stifle a snigger behind him. 'But I thank you for coming.'

'We have his effects.'

'His pipes?' Florence scoffed. 'I suppose I might find a space for them somewhere.' She looked past the inspector to the young man by the graveside. 'Sergeant Graves, you were with him when he died, were you not?'

The normally cheerful Graves looked suddenly solemn. 'That is so,' he nodded as he handed over the box containing Hicks' belongings.

Florence Habgood's voice was quiet. 'Was it... quick?' she asked.

Graves nodded. 'He would not have felt a thing,' he said. He was sure he spoke the truth, but he could not shake the image of the inspector in Callaghan's clutches. He knew the look of animal panic in Hicks' eyes would stay with him a long time. He also knew that it would serve nobody to know if it, particularly Mrs Habgood. 'He will be missed,' the sergeant concluded, simply.

Florence Habgood looked as if she did not believe him.

'Inspector Bowman,' she began, 'I know you and Ignatius had your differences, but he was a good man, no matter how he might have occasionally presented himself.'

'I have no doubt of it,' Bowman offered.

'But the truth of the matter is that he was a man out of his time. The world is changing, and with it Scotland Yard.'

Bowman blinked. He knew Hicks had grown more uncomfortable with the increasing demands of detective work.

'He had, of late, professed a desire to retire from the police force altogether to pursue a quieter life.' A tear sprung again to her eye as she spoke. 'But then, Superintendent Callaghan had invigorated him.' She lifted her gaze from the grave before her. 'A man like my brother desires only to be considered useful, Inspector Bowman. It is a tragedy indeed that the man who finally made him feel of use, also proved to be his end.'

Bowman nodded, unsure why he suddenly felt so guilty. Perhaps it was that, throughout his dealings with the portly inspector, he had failed to really get to know him at all. All too often, Hicks had presented himself as an obstacle, an almost immovable object to be circumnavigated in the course of an investigation. Perhaps Bowman could have tried to be more understanding.

There was an awkward silence as the inspector wondered how best to end the conversation. He could feel Sergeant Graves shuffling awkwardly beside him.

Fortunately, Florence Habgood clearly had no mind for such pleasantries. Tucking the box containing her late brother's effects beneath her arm, she simply turned and walked away.

When she was a safe distance from them, Graves dared to turn to the inspector. 'A pint of porter should make all right,' he grinned. 'We could raise a jar to Hicks.'

Bowman sighed as he looked around. The sun was burning through the cloud and, for a moment, the whole churchyard was bathed in its golden light. Bowman was even sure he could feel its warmth upon his back. 'Good idea, Graves,' he said, at last.

'And perhaps to his sister, too. It is not so easy to be alone in the world.'

They reached the public house just as Mrs Habgood's sombre brougham rattled away. The two men stood for a while to watch it go, then turned to the door. The Fish And Ring seemed a simple enough establishment from the outside, and compact too. The wooden frontage had clearly seen better days, cracked and bleached as it was from exposure to the elements. A bedraggled sign swung stiffly from a hook with a lack of enthusiasm that seemed shared by the drinkers Bowman could see within. He swallowed and hesitated on the threshold. This was the first time he had been near a public house since the events in Larton. In truth, he felt his compulsion to drink had waned, but he wondered if he were playing with fire. He was almost relieved to feel a tug at his elbow.

'Forgive me, sir,' came a voice, 'but can you help me?'

Bowman turned to see the woman with the grey hair from the churchyard. She was shifting nervously from foot to foot. 'I knew that Florence Habgood's brother was to be buried today and that he was a Scotland Yarder. I had hoped there would be some fellow detectives at his funeral. Is that you, sir?'

Sergeant Graves had joined his companion at the kerbside, barely disguising a look of disappointment at being called from the bar by the commotion.

'I am Inspector Bowman and this is Detective Sergeant Graves,' Bowman was saying. 'Did you know Ignatius Hicks?'

The woman shook her head. 'Barely,' she said, 'but then I did not come to pay my respects.'

'Oh?' Bowman shared a look with his sergeant.

'Perhaps you might join us for a drink?' Graves offered, breezily.

The mysterious woman looked shocked at the proposal, her

ruddy cheeks flushing darker still. 'It would not be seemly,' she gasped. 'Besides, I would not wish the details of the case to be made public.'

Bowman's moustache twitched. 'Case?' he echoed, suddenly concerned.

'Are you in danger, Miss - ?'

'Stallard,' the woman whispered. 'Mrs Isabella Stallard.' Bowman noticed she looked around her as she spoke. 'As to whether I am in any danger, that is a matter yet to be resolved.'

'Have you been threatened with violence?' Graves' eyes softened with concern.

'These are the details with which you will be acquainted if you only come with me to my house.'

Now it was Bowman's turn to look about him. 'This is most irregular, Mrs Stallard. We are neither of us on duty.' He gestured to his and his companion's mourning coats.

Mrs Stallard tugged at Bowman's sleeve again. 'But I have not the time to go to Scotland Yard. Matters have come to a head.'

'And the local police - ?' Graves began.

'Are dullards,' Isabella concluded, 'and not to be trusted. I cannot risk my name being connected with anything improper. My reputation is important to me.'

Graves' eyes narrowed in thought. He knew many of London's local police stations were ill run and ill equipped. Perhaps Mrs Stallard was wise to avoid them.

'Very well,' nodded Bowman at last, 'take us to your home and we will hear more.'

Isabella Stallard let go a breath as if a great weight had been taken from her shoulders. 'Thank you, Inspector Bowman. My driver waits with a carriage around the corner.'

Throughout the journey, Sergeant Graves' contrivances to

engage Mrs Stallard in conversation came to nought. His attempts to talk of the weather or the busy streets were ignored, much to Bowman's evident amusement. Mrs Stallard simply gazed from the window, all the while gnawing at her lip.

As the carriage wove its way between gaudy coloured horse-drawn omnibuses on their way to the city and smaller carts laden with lumber, Bowman took an interest in the houses that lined the streets. There were whole streets given over to slums, he saw. They were pressed so tight together that it was almost impossible to discern where one dwelling ended and another began. Their residents spilled out onto the road as if they had been ejected by force, or as if there simply wasn't room enough to hold them all within. Some stumbled in the glare of the low sun, their eyes displaying the vacant stare of the opium addict. Others searched through the detritus that lay by the road for food or clothing or anything that could be sold for a ha'penny. And yet, for all the squalor, Bowman noticed that whole squares of smart townhouses would flash by periodically. Handsome terraces spoke of a burgeoning middle class with the means to afford such property. That they stood cheek by jowl with some of the most deprived and depraved that London had to offer seemed to trouble none of them. As the carriage turned off White Horse Street into York Square, Bowman was presented with a row of smart townhouses, each rendered in a cheery shade of yellow. They rose over five stories and, it seemed, each contended with the other to present as opulent an appearance as possible. Where one had an elaborate portico over the front door, another had a pair of Corinthian columns. Where one had plaster cherubs placed over the windows, another had a collection of saints arranged along its entire front elevation. Where one had a single tree in its front garden, another boasted a collection of exotic ferns.

The carriage slowed and Sergeant Graves leaned forward to

release the door for their fellow passenger. Isabella Stallard disembarked with a grateful nod to the driver who had alighted to guide her to the kerbside with an outstretched hand.

Almost as soon as her foot had touched the pavement, a door swung open in one of the houses before her. As Bowman and Graves alighted from the carriage, they were invited to follow the mysterious lady with a gesture of her hand. Climbing the steps to the front door, Bowman could see he was about to enter a rarefied environment.

The first thing he noticed as he entered the spacious and well-appointed hall, was the silence. As the door was closed behind the two detectives by a rather stout footman, the outside world seemed to retreat. The rattle of the carriages on the main road was banished and the hubbub of everyday life dispelled. The interior of the house seemed an oasis from the hurly burly of the city, and Bowman was left to wonder just what had happened to disturb it.

'Spencer will take your coats,' came Mrs Stallard's voice from a room off the hall.

Bowman looked at a row of framed photographs that hung upon the wall. They showed a rather unprepossessing man standing stiffly with various classes of children. In each of the portraits, they sat cross-legged at the man's feet, staring balefully at the camera.

The footman reached up to relieve Bowman and Graves of their black tailcoats. He was a mean looking man with a pinched mouth and dark, beetle brows. Bowman noticed he regarded them with what could only be described as a well-practised look of disdain.

'You can make your own way into the parlour,' Spencer hissed, waving a heavy arm in the general direction of the interior of the house.

'You're too kind,' Sergeant Graves beamed in response, his

blond curls falling into his eyes.

The footman glowered even more as he turned to hang their coats in a cloakroom under the stairs.

'Don't mind Spencer,' cautioned Mrs Stallard as the two men joined her in the parlour. 'He has not been with us long and is yet to be schooled in the particulars of his position.'

'He certainly has character,' offered Graves with a smile.

'Mrs Stallard,' Bowman interrupted, 'forgive me. I am eager to know the details of your case.'

Isabella Stallard took a breath and gestured to two comfortable chairs set either side of the fireplace. They were upholstered, noticed Bowman, in an exquisite burgundy velveteen. Looking around him as he sat, he saw that every other piece of furniture in the room was equally well-appointed. A walnut writing desk stood by the window, inlaid with a gold trim. Two mahogany bookcases groaned with books and a selection of landscapes lined the walls. A well-stocked fire spat and hissed in the grate.

'I am a member of a local lending library,' Mrs Stallard began as she crossed to the fireplace. 'Every Monday morning, I am delivered of a new book to be read. A runner delivers the new book and takes the old. It is a most successful scheme.' There was a note of excitement in her voice as she spoke. 'So far this year I have read Tolstoy, Thackeray, Bronte and most recently, Hardy. But this morning, I was delivered of this.' Mrs Stallard reached up to the mantelpiece to retrieve a slim, leather-bound volume. Even from his chair, Bowman could see the title; 'A Christmas Carol.'

'It seems most appropriate, with the coming of the season,' said Mrs Stallard.

Bowman blinked. Was it nearly Christmas already? Truth be told, much of the year had passed in a haze. He had spent weeks at a time in a funk, or worse, such that he had not even noticed the passage of time. He had read Dickens' seasonal masterpiece, of course, though he did not think he would ever read it again. Bowman felt he'd had rather enough of vengeful ghosts.

'My husband brought the opened parcel to me from the door and I brought the book into the parlour to begin the reading of it. I know it so well, of course, but look forward to reacquainting myself with Mr Scrooge every year. I sat in your very chair, Inspector Bowman, and opened the book. And this fell out.'

She held an envelope between her slender fingers. Bowman instinctively held out a hand to take it from her.

Sergeant Graves shuffled forwards on his chair to see as Bowman withdrew a piece of paper from the envelope. The inspector passed it to his companion as he examined the envelope.

Graves cleared his throat before he read. 'One thousand pounds upon return of this book will prevent the world knowing of Olivia.'

'Mrs Stallard,' Graves began, carefully. 'Who is Olivia?'

'There you draw close to the matter, Sergeant Graves,' Isabella whispered. 'Olivia is my daughter.'

Bowman shook his head in confusion. 'And what of her?'

No sooner had the words escaped his lips, than Bowman saw a change in the woman's demeanour. It was as if she had been holding back a tide of emotion and suddenly it was free to run its course. Isabella Stallard almost buckled where she stood. If it had not been for Sergeant Graves, who rushed to her side to support her, Bowman was certain she would have fallen to the hearth. The young sergeant led her to his chair and lowered her carefully down.

'Now you will see why I did not wish the local police to know of this matter.' Mrs Stallard dabbed at her eyes with a lace handkerchief, breathing deep as she fought to recover her composure. 'I was delivered of a baby girl when I was aged but seventeen. It is a shame with which I have learned to live, but my family took it hard.'

Bowman swallowed. He could quite understand how such an event might have made its mark upon the poor woman.

'I was sent away to bear the pregnancy in a hospital, permitted to name her only, and then the mite was taken from me.'

Bowman sighed. 'And were you then returned to your family?'

'I was,' Isabella nodded through her tears, 'but I was forbidden to make mention of my daughter. The matter was never spoken of again.'

'Until now.' Graves was holding the note before him.

In the silence that followed, Mrs Stallard rose and moved to the fireplace. With her hand upon the mantel, she stared into the guttering flames as if enlightenment might be found in the grate.

'I hold a certain position in this neighbourhood,' she said quietly. 'I sit on several boards and am a benefactor of the local school. Much of my time is taken up with supporting activities and lessons at St Dunstan's Church. If the matter of my daughter was to be known abroad, my reputation would be dashed at a stroke.'

Graves raised his eyebrows.

'You mistake my concern for hubris, Sergeant Graves,' Mrs Stallard clarified. 'These positions mean nothing more to me other than that they afford me the means to do good work. If I were removed from any of them, I fear my efforts to support the poor in our community would be curtailed.'

Inspector Bowman nodded in understanding. 'Mrs Stallard,' he began, 'do you have any idea who would know of your daughter?'

Mrs Stallard shook her head, emphatically. 'Not in London, certainly. But in Norfolk…'

Bowman frowned as he tried to follow her train of thought.

'Norfolk?'

Just as Mrs Stallard opened her mouth to respond, there came a noise from the hall.

'Ah, Spencer,' came a voice. 'I am glad to be out of the cold.'

Mrs Stallard stood back from the fireplace in anticipation of the newcomer.

'Mrs Stallard is in the parlour,' growled Spencer from the hall. 'With her guests.'

There was a silence.

'Guests?'

Bowman heard the footman attempting to lower his voice. 'Detectives,' he rasped, 'from Scotland Yard.'

There was a flurry of activity from the hall and, suddenly, a man appeared at the door. He cut a slight figure, Bowman saw. A rather bookish appearance was enhanced by the man's prominent forehead, thick-lensed spectacles and rather bemused expression. Inspector Bowman recognised him at once as the man from the photographs in the hallway.

'Archibald, dear,' Mrs Stallard smiled.

'Isabella, my dove,' the man twitched. 'I see we have visitors.'

The two detectives rose from their seats to make their introductions. Bowman was particularly struck by the man's weak handshake and the softness of his skin.

'This is my husband,' Mrs Stallard elucidated.

Archibald licked his lips. 'My dear,' he began, 'I thought we had agreed not to call upon the police.'

Isabella managed a polite smile. 'We agreed not to call upon the *local* police. I knew Florence Habgood was to bury her brother today.'

'The detective?' Archibald blinked.

'Indeed,' Isabella nodded. 'I hoped a colleague or two would be in attendance, and so it proved.' She gestured towards the two men standing awkwardly before her. 'Inspector Bowman and Sergeant Graves were good enough to look into the matter of the note.'

Archibald looked suddenly flustered. 'You have told them of the note?' he squealed.

Bowman felt the time had come to intercede. 'Blackmail is a criminal matter, Mr Stallard.'

'It is also a private matter, Inspector Bowman.'

Bowman detected a note of steel behind the man's words.

'Clearly, your wife does not agree,' Graves offered with a disarming smile.

Mr Stallard turned to his wife in agitation. 'I thought we had agreed to pay the money. We can certainly afford a thousand pounds.'

'That is easy to say when it is not your money.'

Mrs Stallard's icy response cut the air and left her husband flushing almost as red as his wife. Embarrassed, Bowman averted his gaze and looked around the room. His eyes fell upon the fine Chinawear displayed in a cabinet by the door.

'Family money, inspector,' Isabella said suddenly. '*My* family money.' Archibald blushed again.

'Then your family forgave you?' Graves asked, bravely.

'Just how much have you told them?' stuttered Archibald.

'If they are to investigate this note, they must know everything,' Isabella replied a note of calm acceptance in her voice.

In response, Archibald Stallard marched stiffly to a bureau and poured himself a drink from a decanter that stood among a collection of cut crystal glasses.

Isabella turned to the inspector. 'My maiden name is Latchford, Inspector Bowman, and my family hail from Norfolk. You might well have heard of them.'

Bowman's forehead creased into his habitual frown as he

thought. 'Latchford's mustard?' he asked. Graves' eyes widened as Isabella Stallard nodded in confirmation.

'Indeed,' Isabella nodded. 'Perhaps now you see why my condition could not be tolerated. My father's company was founded upon the principles of a family business. You can well imagine how my falling pregnant at so early an age threatened to undermine his reputation.'

Bowman nodded. There was that word, again. He noticed Archibald downing his drink more quickly than was seemly.

Sergeant Graves cleared his throat. 'You said you believed only someone in Norfolk would know of your daughter? Family, perhaps?'

Isabella shook her head. 'I have no family now, Sergeant Graves. Both my parents are long gone and I am their only child.'

'Then the company?' Bowman asked carefully.

'It was sold to a competitor upon their deaths,' Mrs Stallard explained.

Bowman nodded. That would at least explain why the Stallards lived in such comfort, and perhaps why they had this morning become a target.

'It is my opinion,' interjected Archibald, emboldened by brandy, 'that we should pay up and let that make an end of the matter.'

'And if they ask for more?' rounded Isabella. 'Or make my story public anyway? You may have no reputation to defend outside of Whitstable, Archibald, but my name carries a greater weight. I will not see it sullied.' Archibald Stallard spluttered in exasperation.

'You were a teacher at Whitstable?' asked Bowman.

Graves couldn't help but be impressed at his superior's assertion.

'I saw the pictures in the hall,' the detective inspector

continued by way of explanation.

'You are most observant,' Archibald hissed as he downed the last of his drink. 'Well, inspector, as you are here, what do you suggest?'

There was a silence as Bowman thought. 'Mrs Stallard, might I take this book and the note?'

'Of course,' Isabella nodded.

'Then I shall ask Sergeant Graves to make some enquiries at the lending library.' He passed the volume to his colleague. 'The address is written on the first page.' The sergeant nodded. 'They may at least shed some light on how the note was placed in the book, and from there we may discover who wrote it.'

'That is all?' Archibald Stallard stood blinking by the bureau.

'What more would you have us do?' Inspector Bowman asked, politely.

'You see, my dove?' Archibald had turned to his wife, appealing to her with open hands. 'Scotland Yard are no better than amateurs. It is a folly to have involved them.'

Isabella Stallard chose to ignore her husband and turned instead to call the footman.

'Would you show the gentlemen out, Spencer?' she asked, calmly. With curt nods of thanks, the detectives allowed themselves to be led to the hall, whereupon they were reunited with their coats.

'Just how long have you been in the Stallards' employ, Spencer?' Bowman asked with an affected air of nonchalance.

'Two years,' the footman grumbled as if it was of no concern to any but himself. 'Mrs Stallard brought me here shortly after she married.'

Bowman raised his eyebrows. He had imagined the Stallards had been married longer.

With that, Spencer bustled them out the door into the grey street beyond, but not before Inspector Bowman had taken a closer look at the photographs on the wall. As they walked gingerly down the steps to the road, the two detectives could hear voices rising from the house behind them. Mr and Mrs Stallard were clearly continuing the argument without them.

The Fish And Ring was as welcoming a public house as would be imagined from its fading exterior. Inside, paint peeled from the woodwork and almost every surface seemed given over to proud displays of cobwebs and dust.

Sergeant Graves grimaced as he took the first sip of his ale. A bitter aftertaste caused his face to crease in so comedic a manner that Bowman couldn't help but laugh.

'And I was so looking forward to it,' Graves grumbled.

'It does not always pay to stray far from what you know,' smiled Bowman as he raised his glass of porter. 'To Inspector Hicks,' he said.

Graves nodded, suddenly serious. 'To Hicks,' he repeated, and he steeled himself for another sip.

'What'll you do next, sir?' the young sergeant asked as he wiped a moustache of foam from his upper lip.

'I wish to know more of Archibald Stallard,' the inspector breathed. 'I would ask you to begin your investigation at the lending library. See if anyone there might have knowledge of Mrs Stallard's past and the inclination to use it against her.'

Graves nodded, enthusiastically. He was never happier than in the course of an investigation. He was happier still that Inspector Bowman was, once again, at its head. 'And you, sir?'

Bowman gulped at his porter. 'I shall find my way home first, to change.' He indicated his sombre, black coat and wing-collared shirt. 'And then, I will treat myself to some bracing sea air.'

The train was as empty as Bowman had expected. Day-trippers were in short supply in November and a holiday by the coast was the last thing on anyone's mind. The inspector gazed through the window as the great tender heaved its way along the London, Chatham and Dover Railway. Soon, the capital city was little more than a greasy smudge on the horizon, and the open vista before him was broken only by country roads and isolated farms. Every now and then, a small village would hove into view, only to flash past in an instant and be replaced by a grey-brown patchwork of fields. The harvest was long since done and now they stood barren, awaiting the promise of spring.

As he settled back in his seat, he saw the light was already fading, even though it was only mid-afternoon. He did not care for the winter gloom that lay ahead. Soon, lulled by the movement of the carriage upon the rails, Bowman's head nodded onto his chest and he dozed lightly for the remainder of his journey. Dartford, Rainham, Sittingbourne and Faversham all passed unnoticed.

All too soon, he felt himself jolted to his senses by the arrival into Whitstable. As the guard on the platform blew his whistle, Bowman stepped from the footplate and onto the long, low platform. The station, he noticed, was gaily painted and festooned with the remnants of summer. Posters invited visitors to 'Take The Sea Air!' or 'Stroll About The Town!' There were signs to the harbour and the sea front. Just three months previously, Bowman was certain he would not have been, as he was now, the only passenger to disembark. Swinging the carriage door shut behind him, he stepped back as the engine gave a hiss and made his way to the main entrance. As the train rolled from the station on its journey to the Kent coast and the channel ports, Bowman fancied he could smell the sea.

The Thames Estuary was wide here at Whitstable but on a clear day, the observant visitor could make out the coast of Essex, squatting low on the horizon. The pretty town had much to recommend it, even on this particular autumn afternoon. Turning up his collar, Bowman passed into the pretty High Street, the train having delivered him straight to the heart of the town. Shops and houses painted in pretty pastels stood back from the road, their summer wares replaced with the provisions needed only by the town's inhabitants. The bakers and grocery shops were quiet now, their owners happy to see their way through the winter on the profits they had made in the summer months.

Bowman followed the map he had committed to memory back in his rooms at Hampstead, and within a quarter of an hour or so, found himself at his destination. Whitstable and Seasalter Endowed Church of England School stood behind an impressive pair of wrought iron gates halfway up the High Street. Situated in the very heart of the little community, it was built of red brick and flint, its high walls punctuated with tall windows designed to allow as much light as possible to fall upon the little scholars within. As Bowman approached the entrance, he could hear the strains of a hymn drifting from the hall to his right. Young voices strained to reach the heights of 'We Plough The Fields And Scatter' as a piano was hammered to the limits of its tolerance. Pulling at the bell, Bowman straightened his coat about him and the door swung open.

The school secretary was a severe looking woman with her hair scraped back into a bun. Indeed, thought Bowman, it was pinned back so severely that he fancied the poor woman had difficulty blinking. Her cheeks shone as if they had been freshly scrubbed, and her mouth was framed with a pair of lips so thin that they were barely lips at all.

'I am Detective Inspector Bowman from Scotland Yard.'

The woman blinked as best she could, clearly taken aback at

the announcement.

'Might I come in?'

'On what business?' The woman asked, her nasal voice laced with suspicion.

Bowman threw his hands wide. 'I have a few questions regarding a former employee, that is all.' He looked the woman up and down. She was in her later years and dressed all in black. A large skirt hid her feet entirely from view and a shawl was draped across her shoulders. She wrung her hands together as she spoke, though Bowman could not discern whether as an attempt to stave off the cold or as a sign of anxiety.

'Which employee?' she asked.

Bowman cleared his throat, suddenly wondering if the journey had been a waste of time. 'Mr Archibald Stallard.'

The change in the woman's demeanour was marked. At the mention of Stallard's name, she stiffened. Her hands fell to her side and she suddenly looked about her as if wary of being overheard. At last, she huffed, rolled her eyes at the inconvenience, then gestured that the inspector should accompany her inside.

'I am Evadne Beckett,' the woman announced as she led Inspector Bowman into her tiny office. 'I have been secretary here at Whitstable and Seasalter for fifteen years, inspector. And yes, I remember Mr Stallard very well, indeed.'

She motioned that Bowman should sit in the chair opposite her desk. It was hard and unforgiving. It would not have surprised Bowman if the lack of comfort was a deliberate design. Mrs Beckett did not seem the type to relish company. Around him, shelves were lined with ledgers and folders of papers. Each was labelled and placed in order. A calendar hung upon the wall marked with the important dates in the school term. The office, thought Bowman, rather like the woman before him, seemed the very model of efficiency.

'When was Mr Stallard employed here?' Bowman asked, settling back into his chair.

'I can tell you exactly, inspector,' replied Mrs Beckett with a note of pride in her voice. She made her way to a particular shelf and ran her finger along it, looking at the labels fixed to each of the ledgers. Bowman noticed she made a peculiar clicking noise with her tongue as she concentrated. At last, she withdrew a ledger and slapped it on her desk with great ceremony. Lowering herself into her chair, a much more comfortable affair than Bowman's, he noticed, she licked a finger and proceeded to flick through the pages before her.

'Mr Stallard joined us on the twelfth of March Eighteen Hundred and Eighty Four,' she announced. She turned over several pages and traced her finger along a line of neatly written text. Bowman had no doubt it was her own. 'He left us five years later, on the twenty third of June, Eighteen Eighty Nine.'

Bowman frowned. Then the Stallards had only been resident in London for three years.

'Under what circumstances?'

At this, Mrs Beckett rose to shut the door. 'A scandal, Inspector Bowman, that very nearly saw an end to the school.'

Bowman leaned forward in his chair as the school secretary returned to her desk. 'Go on,' he implored.

'Mr Stallard's marriage was not a happy one,' Mrs Beckett said, slowly. Bowman noted she was choosing her words with deliberate care. 'The Stallards joined us from Sussex where he had been employed as a history teacher. At first, he showed great promise here, but soon it was discovered he had been making use of school funds for his own use.'

'In what way?'

'His wife had succumbed to a dreadful addiction. A series of them, in fact. There was talk of opium and the stronger spirits,'

Bowman blinked. If that had been the case just three years ago, then Mrs Stallard had clearly made a startling recovery. The lady he had met in Stepney seemed possessed of a most indomitable nature. But then, he knew from personal experience, such a recovery was not entirely impossible.

'It seems,' Mrs Beckett continued, sadly, 'that she stole the means to sustain her habits from her husband. So much so, that they fell behind in their rent. They kept rooms in a house by the harbour, inspector. We keep several properties around the town for our staff, a legacy of a particularly generous benefactor. Of course, the bursar soon noticed when the rent failed to appear in the school accounts each month.' Bowman nodded. 'Our bursar is a fastidious man, Inspector Bowman, and he took it upon himself to conduct a full audit of the school's finances.' Mrs Beckett leaned forward over the desk, her voice low. 'He discovered that someone had been taking the school pence over a period of several months.'

Bowman's moustache twitched. He knew the 'school pence' to be the money paid by the richer families to send their children to school. As well as going some way towards paying for the staff and necessary facilities, it also subsidised the poorer children. One of the greatest developments of the modern age, thought Bowman, was the opening up of education to all classes until the age of ten. Perhaps, in time, it might benefit the Empire greatly to have a better educated populace.

'Did Mr Stallard admit to it?'

'Almost immediately,' Mrs Beckett nodded. 'The board was then tasked with the question of the consequences he should face.'

'And what was their conclusion?'

Mrs Beckett held Bowman in her gaze. The inspector noticed her mouth looked meaner than ever. 'That we should not go to the authorities.'

Bowman sighed. If Commissioner Bradford were here, he would surely have despaired.

'Why would you not consider involving the police if there was clear evidence of a crime?'

Mrs Beckett hesitated before responding. 'We had our reputation to consider,' she said, finally.

Bowman nodded. He had been hearing that word rather a lot of late.

'We are a much respected institution in Whitstable, and much of our income depends upon us remaining so. We have many generous benefactors in the town and, frankly, without them we could not maintain the standards of which we are so proud. To be publicly exposed to such scandal by way of a police investigation would ruin us.' She shook her head, vehemently. 'The town would never forgive us if they learned we had employed a man whose wife had fallen so low. We hold ourselves to higher standards.'

Bowman bit his lip. He had often heard such judgements levied against those who were deemed to have lapsed in some way. They were most often in want of means, and they were most often women.

'So Mr Stallard was let go?'

The secretary nodded. 'Quite so. It was clear he could not afford to pay back the money he had taken.'

Satisfied with the matter, Bowman rose from the chair and knocked his hat into shape. As she led him to the door, Mrs Beckett couldn't help but be intrigued as to the purpose of the inspector's visit.

'Why do you need to know of Mr Stallard, inspector?' she asked. 'I hope that Scotland Yard is not intent upon pursuing our case against him?'

'Not at all,' replied Bowman, thoughtfully. 'We are

investigating another matter that concerns him. One in which it appears he and his wife are the victims.'

Mrs Beckett seemed to soften a little. 'I am sorry to hear it,' she whispered. 'But are they otherwise well?'

Bowman turned to her, touched by her concern. 'They are.'

Mrs Beckett nodded in thanks. 'For all that happened here, I would not wish Mrs Stallard ill. I understand she spent some time in the Victoria Hospital in Folkestone but I am glad to hear she is recovered. She was quite the celebrity around the harbour.'

Bowman paused with his hand on the door. 'Celebrity?'

Mrs Beckett allowed herself a little laugh, in spite of herself. 'Certainly. We are quite used to the Bohemian type in Whitstable, Inspector Bowman. There is many a painter finds their way to our town on account of the light, and many a poet and writer on account of the sea. But still, Mrs Stallard stood apart.' Encouraged by Bowman's look, she continued in her reverie. 'She had better days than others,' she said, wistfully, 'and on those better days she might be found painting by the harbour wall.'

'Really?' Bowman was thinking hard. There had been no indication in York Square that Mrs Stallard was an artist.

'Oh yes, inspector. She was quite the picture herself with her flame red hair and Bohemian dress.'

Bowman took a breath. 'Red hair?'

'She was a natural beauty,' added Mrs Beckett, warming to her theme. 'I always thought there was something of the Irish about her, with her pale skin and all.'

Inspector Bowman allowed himself to be let to the school entrance whereupon he offered his thanks to the school secretary. As he swung the wrought iron gates closed behind him, Bowman fought to gather his thoughts. He leaned against the wall and took a deep draft of the sea air. Mrs Beckett's description of Archibald's wretched wife didn't sound like Isabella Stallard at all.

The guest house was comfortable enough. Reasoning that it was too late an hour to return to London, Inspector Bowman had walked about the harbour then secured a room for the night at The Black Dog, a cosy public house on the High Street. By standing at an angle, he found he could see the sea from his window. He stood for some time, letting his eyes travel the length of the horizon as the last light of the day faded to an inky black. Then, resolving to be up early enough to catch the first train in the morning, he splashed his face in the basin of water on the washstand and readied himself for bed.

As he drifted off to sleep, one thing continued to puzzle him. If Archibald Stallard had left Whitstable and Seasalter under such a cloud of disgrace, why did he so brazenly display a photograph of himself outside the school in his hall in York Square? Could it be that the present Mrs Stallard had no knowledge of her husband's previous misadventures?

Detective Sergeant Anthony Graves was in his element. As long as he had a task in hand, he was happy enough. Even the dour November weather could not shake his natural exuberance. Having concluded his enquiries at the lending library, he turned his thoughts and heels towards Stepney Green with the thought of catching a train back to the city. He had satisfied himself that there was no one at the library with any connection to the Stallards, less still with any inclination to subject them to the ignominy of blackmail. Likewise, he could not imagine that the note could have been placed into the book prior to dispatch. It seemed the books were picked entirely at random. Indeed, the defining feature of the library's home lending service was that the reader would be continually surprised by the matter presented to them. Graves could see no joy in reading someone else's fiction. He was sure no author alive could compete with what the young sergeant had seen in his life. Fact was, indeed, almost always stranger than fiction.

Continuing his investigations, Graves had found the lad who delivered the books had no capacity for writing, let alone anything more than a passing acquaintance with Mrs Stallard. Perhaps, the sergeant reasoned, the note had been placed by person or persons unknown when the boy was otherwise distracted by his deliveries. But then, Mrs Stallard had mentioned the book being delivered as a parcel. How then, had the note been positioned within the book and under its wrapping?

The librarian had given Sergeant Graves directions to the station and so he walked, his head down against the wind, through the bustling streets of Stepney. It was a part of London with which he was not familiar, and he was surprised to see so many people of different stations of life mixing so freely. The smartest shops catered for the smarter clientele that Graves could see about him; gentlemen in silk top hats and fur trimmed coats escorting well-dressed ladies from their carriages to do their shopping. The drivers would remain at the roadside as the ladies went about their business, napping on their perches while their horses shifted impatiently in their harnesses. The professional classes bustled this way and that with their Gladstone bags on their way to some meeting or other. They tripped up steps to push at doors decorated with brass plaques proclaiming the presence of some doctor, lawyer or broker within. All around them, the less fortunate attempted to scrape a living. Stallholders and traders competed with each other, calling to the passers by that they should sample their wares over some other's. Chestnuts were roasted over braziers at street corners, shoes were shined by the entrance to Stepney Junction.

And then, came the dissolute. Those without employment loitered in the entrances to churchyards and formal gardens, half-empty bottles in their hands. Shoeless urchins scampered between the legs of the shoppers or badgered the shopkeepers for charity, their grimy hands held up in supplication. Above all this, Graves glimpsed the towers of the nearby gas works looming over the rooftops. All human life and all human industry, it seemed, was to be found in Stepney.

Graves had noticed the quality of housing drop as he walked, from the smart town houses of York Square, to the ramshackle slums he saw before him. It seemed impossible that such extremes could exist within a mile of each other. It might as well have been a different world.

The houses were crammed together as if they were fighting for space. The brickwork shone with grease and soot, the glassless windows gaped liked empty eye sockets. Rubbish spewed from doors and into the street. The people in their rags were difficult to discern from the debris on the road. Graves felt his ire rise as he considered how others might profit from such misery. Each of these unfortunate wretches had to pay for the privilege of living in such squalor. Commonly, one among them was elected bailiff to collect the rent, often with menaces. Those who couldn't pay would be ejected without ceremony to fend for themselves. Deprived of shelter at this time of year, they would be dead within weeks.

Just as Graves prepared to cross the road, he noticed a figure walking with purpose on the pavement opposite. Sinking back into a doorway, he watched as Archibald Stallard turned into Hope Place, treading carefully through the detritus on the road. As carriages rattled past, Graves strained to keep his quarry in sight. Only when he was sure Stallard would not turn and notice him did he cross the road, dodging an oncoming brougham and a chimney sweep with his cart. Ducking into the gloom, he pressed himself against a crumbling wall to watch as Stallard made his way along the row of filthy tenements. Eyes gazed up from the roadside as he stepped gingerly through a knot of children, their filthy faces as black as coal. He even paused once or twice to acknowledge the greetings of one or two of the residents, although Sergeant Graves noticed their forced smiles would disappear just as soon as Stallard had passed. At last, he disappeared through a door.

Graves quickened his step, feeling suddenly conspicuous in his formal coat and tie. As he neared the house where he had seen Stallard disappear, he fancied he heard voices from an upper window. A woman's hysterical screams pierced the air while two men - Graves was certain one of them was Stallard - sought to quieten her. Then the two men seemed to argue amongst themselves. Though the words were indistinct, the passion that lay behind them was apparent enough. The altercation rose in volume until there came a noise like the crash of falling furniture. Suddenly, there was silence.

Just as Graves gathered himself to investigate, he heard the woman again. This time, she was sobbing uncontrollably. Her keening drifted to the street below as Stallard suddenly appeared at the door. Sergeant Graves noticed he was trying to hide a bloodied nose as he turned to walk briskly back to the main road. Turning up his collar, Graves watched him go for a while, then crossed the street to investigate.

The door had no latch and so swung open at a touch. Peering into the passageway beyond, Graves found himself a subject of interest. Several pairs of eyes glared threateningly from the gloom.

'What d'ya want?' came a voice. The smell of stale tobacco and the tang of urine assailed Graves' nostrils.

'Who among you knows Archibald Stallard?' the sergeant

129

asked, boldly.

'What business is it of yours?'

Graves recognised the other voice he had heard from the window, arguing with Stallard. It belonged to a burly man dressed in a tattered shirt and waistcoat. A scarf about his neck was his only concession to the cold.

'I am Sergeant Graves from Scotland Yard,' announced Graves, and he heard the shuffling of feet as those around him scampered from the passageway in alarm.

'There's nothing here for a mutton shunter,' the burly man insisted, rolling up his sleeves.

'I heard an altercation,' persisted Graves. 'I wish only to be of assistance.'

'Then be of assistance somewhere else.'

Graves was suddenly aware that the other residents had returned. This time, they were each of them armed with makeshift weapons. Lengths of wood, tools and strips of metal were held menacingly before them. Even in the failing light of the afternoon, their intentions were clear on their faces.

'Tell Stallard I will expose him if he resists,' the man growled and, at a signal, he set his mob upon the young sergeant.

As one who gives himself up to the swell of the tide the better to be carried to safety, so Graves suffered to be carried to the street by the throng around him. Save a blow or two to the head and some pinches about the arms, he emerged unscathed onto Hope Place. Finding purchase against the filth in the road, he made good his escape with nothing damaged but his pride, the baying mob cheering in triumph at his retreating back.

'You wouldn't have stood a chance,' agreed Bowman over a breakfast of kippers.

The Silver Cross was busy, even at this early hour. To his credit, Harris the landlord had cultivated a loyal clientele that stretched beyond the detectives from Scotland Yard. Looking around him, Bowman noticed the butcher from the shop across the road was sharing a morning draft with the new barmaid, a sweet mouse of a girl with knowing eyes and a turned up nose. In a corner, a quorum of white-bearded bankers was conducting business over plates of devilled kidneys. Nearby, a carriage driver in fine livery fortified himself against the cold with a stiff warmer.

Bowman had caught the early train from Whitstable and had been surprised to find himself in the company of a gaggle of commuters with barely a spare seat to be found. As a consequence, he had stood for much of the journey and so had flopped with relief into the vacant chair by the fire at The Silver Cross, certain that he would meet Sergeant Graves there in time.

Sure enough, the young sergeant had appeared presently, full of news from the day before concerning his adventures at Hope Place.

'So you are none the wiser as to just what Stallard was up to?'

Graves' curls swung about his eyes as he shook his head. 'Not a jot, sir,' he confessed as he scooped a helping of liver and onions onto his fork. 'All I gained was a bruise or two for my pains.'

Bowman took a mouthful of kipper. As ever, it was perfectly cooked. It was little wonder, he mused, that The Silver Cross was so popular.

His thoughts were interrupted by the landlord himself. Harris sauntered over to the table with a jar of ale for the inspector. His lank hair fell into his eyes as he leaned over the table.

'May I offer my condolences on the death of Inspector Hicks?' he said, his leathery skin shining in the light from the fire.

'He'll be missed,' offered Graves as he wiped his mouth on

his sleeve.

'He'll certainly be missed here,' concurred Harris with a rueful smile. 'I'm of a mind to name a beer after him.'

Bowman smiled back. 'That would be a fitting epitaph, indeed, Harris.'

Harris bent so close to Bowman's ear that the inspector could feel his hot breath on his neck. 'Breakfast is on the house, Inspector Bowman. As a sign of my appreciation.' He smiled a toothy smile.

Sergeant Graves raised his glass, a wide grin upon his face and Bowman nodded his thanks.

'Perks of the job,' said Graves as the landlord retreated to the bar. 'What luck did you have in Whitstable, sir?'

Bowman swallowed his mouthful and pushed his empty plate away. 'There is more to Mr Stallard than meets the eye, Graves.' He leaned in closer over the table, delighting in the warmth from the fire. 'It seems he has been married before.'

Graves' eyes grew wide at the news.

'He was dismissed from his previous employment for embezzling funds to support her more unsavoury habits.'

'Do you think the present Mrs Stallard knows?' Graves pushed himself back from the table to stretch his legs.

'We shall find out soon enough, Sergeant Graves.'

Graves was looking thoughtful. 'What became of the first Mrs Stallard, sir?'

Bowman's eyes narrowed at the tone in Graves' voice. It was a tone he knew well. 'The school secretary was given to understand she spent some time in a hospital in Folkestone.'

Graves nodded as he rose to grab their coats from the hook by the chimney breast. 'I have a feeling I might know where she is now.'

The journey to Stepney was frustratingly slow. The cab driver had opted to travel east via The Strand and Fleet Street, only to be confronted with an upturned carriage at St Paul's. There was chaos all around as a result, and the driver was forced to steer his horse into the side streets around Castle Baynard to make any progress. Bowman set his face against the cold and considered the facts with which he had been presented. Despite his protestations, it seemed Graves' visit to Hope Place had paid dividends. It appeared that Mr Stallard hadn't been as honest as he might have been. As the two detectives were carried at last through the streets of Stepney, another question was bothering the inspector. Just when was the note placed in the book?

The hansom rattled into York Square at some considerable speed, and Bowman made a point of thanking the driver for making up the time. As the inspector removed the wooden flap from his lap to step to the pavement, Graves leaned over to snap it shut behind him.

'I'll have the driver take me to Stepney Green Police Station,' he called. 'I have a feeling I'll need the assistance.'

'Very good, Graves,' nodded Bowman. 'Be careful.'

Graves gave his most winning smile and gestured to the driver to proceed. With a snap of his whip, the horses strained against their harnesses and soon the young sergeant had disappeared from sight.

Bowman turned to the house before him. Treading lightly up the steps, he pulled at the bell, almost certain he was being watched from the parlour window.

Once again, he was greeted by the surly footman.

'Might I be admitted to see Mr and Mrs Stallard?' Bowman asked, his moustache twitching almost comically. 'I have a book to return.' He held the copy of 'A Christmas Carol' before him.

Before the footman could answer, Mrs Stallard appeared in the hallway behind him. Her steel grey hair lay loose about her ears. From the redness of her eyes, Bowman guessed she had not slept well that night.

'Have you made progress in the case, Inspector Bowman?' There was a note of hope in her voice that Bowman found almost touching.

'Is your husband at home, Mrs Stallard?' he asked as Spencer relieved him of his coat.

'He will be shortly. Then you have news?'

Bowman swallowed hard. He was not looking forward to this. Mrs Stallard gestured that he would follow her into the parlour and the two sat facing each other by the fire. He placed the book and its contents on a small table beside him.

'What does your husband do for employment, Mrs Stallard?' Bowman asked. The woman opposite him sat poised in the chair, as if in readiness of some revelation.

'He is a private tutor to some of the richer families in Stepney.' She wrung her hands together as she spoke.

Bowman nodded as he looked around the room. Surely, he mused, Stallard's income would barely pay for the heating. 'Then he has no substantial means of his own?'

'I am content to bear the costs our lifestyle incurs, inspector,' Mrs Stallard snapped, impatiently. 'Archibald earns his money, such as it is. I have done nothing to deserve mine.'

'How did you meet?'

A flush rose to Isabella Stallard's cheeks. 'What is the purpose of these questions beyond the wasting of time?'

Bowman cleared his throat, suddenly uncomfortable. 'Mrs Stallard,' he began, 'I have an almost complete picture of what has happened here. It is your place to provide the final pieces to the puzzle.'

Mrs Stallard sighed, resigned.

'I met Archibald at a meeting in support of St Dunstan's. I was keen that the church should provide more assistance for the poor of Stepney. I proposed a fund in support of the needy.'

'In your name?'

Mrs Stallard gave a half smile. 'In my family's name.'

Bowman smiled.

'They failed me in my hour of need, inspector,' Mrs Stallard continued. 'I enjoyed the irony of using their name to give aid to those who needed it.' Mrs Stallard held her chin high, a note of pride in her voice as she spoke. 'The Latchford Fund has provided the people of Stepney with almost two thousand pounds and, I believe, almost certainly saved lives. Spencer was one of them. I found him beneath the bridge at Stepney Green, destitute. I grew to know him a trustworthy fellow, and so offered him a position in my home at once.'

Bowman frowned. Mrs Stallard, it seemed, trusted all too easily.

'And what was Mr Stallard's place in this?'

Isabella shrugged. 'He volunteered to administer the fund,' she said, simply. 'To receive and consider applications and distribute money where appropriate.'

Bowman's eyes narrowed. It would be worth investigating those records, he thought to himself.

'Archibald had just moved from Whitstable where he had gained a reputation of being a most trustworthy teacher.'

Bowman's eyebrows rose. 'Really?'

'His references were excellent,' Mrs Stallard nodded, vigorously. And probably forged, thought Bowman. 'I had no hesitation in appointing him to the position of Administrator to The Latchford Fund.' Her eyes took on a wistful look. 'We spent much time in each other's company, inspector, and grew to know each other completely. I confessed such things to him as I had never confessed to anyone before.'

'Concerning your daughter?' Bowman swallowed. It was clear Isabella Stallard had been completely taken in with her husband. He wasn't looking forward to disabusing her of her opinion.

Isabella smiled. 'He proposed just six months later, and I was proud to become his wife.'

The silence was palpable. Mrs Stallard caught a look in Bowman's eye.

'What is it, inspector?'

Bowman swallowed. 'Mrs Stallard,' he began, cautiously, 'I do not believe you know the full story.'

A look of defiance blazed in Mrs Stallard's eyes. 'And you do?' she asked.

Bowman nodded. 'I believe so. And I also know who is responsible for that note.'

Mrs Stallard took a breath, her hand fluttering about her neck in agitation. 'Who?'

'Your husband.'

There was another silence and Bowman felt his skin begin to flush. Mrs Stallard's eyes burned with indignation.

'Spencer!' she called, at last. 'Would you see that Inspector Bowman is escorted from the house?' She rose from her chair, quivering with fury. 'I will not have my husband impugned within these walls.'

As Bowman stood, he felt Spencer hovering menacingly at the door.

'You must hear me out,' the inspector pleaded. 'I spent much of yesterday at Whitstable, at the school where your husband was a teacher.'

Isabella turned from the window, her eyes brimming with tears. 'You have been investigating Archibald?'

'Mrs Stallard,' said Bowman bravely as Spencer loped into the room, 'your husband already has a wife.'

Time seemed to stop. Bowman peered harder at the lady by the fireplace. Had she stopped breathing? He felt Spencer clutch him by the arm.

'Leave him, Spencer,' Mrs Stallard snapped. 'That'll be all.'

The stout footman released his hold with a glare and retreated reluctantly from the room.

'I am assuming you have evidence for your claim?' Isabella Stallard hissed.

Bowman nodded. 'I do. And I believe there is a direct link between your husband's marriage and the threat of blackmail you received yesterday.'

Mrs Stallard threw her hands to her face. 'This is beyond belief!' she cried, lowering herself again to the chair.

'I am sorry to present you with such news,' Bowman soothed as he moved to offer her such comfort as he could. 'But I believe you deserve to know the truth.'

Mrs Stallard had turned her face to the fire, impassive. Her teeth were clenched and her eyes squeezed shut. It was as if she was preparing herself for a physical blow.

Bowman thought it best to lay all the facts before her. 'Whilst in Whitstable,' he began, quietly, 'I learned that your husband was married to another. She was known about the town as a Bohemian artist. She had fallen into several costly addictions, all of which led to Mr Stallard embezzling money from The Whitstable And Seasalter School.'

Mrs Stallard opened her eyes. 'He speaks of his time there with such pride,' she whispered, as if to herself.

'He was discovered and dismissed,' Bowman countered, softly.

'Then what became of her?'

Bowman swallowed hard. 'The school secretary understood she was being held in a hospital in Folkestone.'

'But you know otherwise?' A look of dread had clouded Mrs Stallard's features. Her cheeks, usually so ruddy, were drained of all colour.

'Mrs Stallard,' Bowman continued, his heart pounding in his chest, 'I believe your husband's wife has been installed in a house just streets away, in Hope Place.'

Isabella Stallard's eyes grew wide in disbelief. 'Here?' she keened. 'In Stepney?' She rose and walked to the window, fixing her eyes on the dreary street beyond.

Bowman nodded. 'Just so. Which brings me to the matter of the blackmailing.'

'Do not trouble yourself, Inspector Bowman,' said Mrs Stallard, suddenly. 'My husband is at the door. You may ask him yourself.'

There came a noise from the hall as Spencer opened the door to the master of the house. Bowman blanched.

'Isabella, dear!' Archibald called. 'I am home!' Bowman could bear the rustle of material as he was relieved of his coat and hat by the footman.

'Mrs Stallard is in the parlour, sir,' came Spencer's reply, heavy with meaning. 'With the inspector.'

The movement stopped. Inspector Bowman had the distinct impression that Archibald Stallard was steeling himself before continuing to the parlour. At last, he stood in the doorway, his chest puffed out in defiance. Gone was the bookish demeanour, to be replaced by a glowering, threatening countenance. He reminded Bowman of a cornered animal.

'Archibald,' began Mrs Stallard, twisting her handkerchief nervously in her hands, 'tell me it isn't true.'

'What's that, my dove?' Archibald replied, one eye on the inspector. He moved cautiously to the window, his arms outstretched in entreaty. Worryingly, Mrs Stallard turned away. 'Tell me of Hope Place,' she rasped.

Archibald stopped mid-stride. Bowman noticed his shoulders slump. A look of defeat settled upon his face. He raised a hand to his brow, wondering how best to proceed, then turned to the inspector by the fire.

'You know of her?' he asked, quietly.

Bowman nodded.

Archibald's hands fell to his side. 'I could not desert her,' he pleaded to his wife's back. 'I could not renege on the oath I took at our wedding.'

'For richer or for poorer?' scoffed Isabella with not a little venom.

Stallard shook his head. 'In sickness and in health.'

'You brought your wife with you from Whitstable.' Bowman interjected.

Archibald nodded, sadly. 'Then you have been to the school?'

'I have.' Bowman's moustache was twitching. 'And there I learned of your wife's…' he searched for the word. 'Frailties.'

Archibald smiled ruefully at the euphemism. 'She is a sick woman, Inspector Bowman. Which of us could leave a loved one in such a condition?'

'But,' Isabella sniffed, turning to him now, 'are you still married to her?'

Archibald did his wife the service of meeting her gaze. He nodded.

Isabella collapsed upon him in her grief, her hands beating pathetically at his chest. 'Oh, Archibald,' she wailed. 'Then our marriage means nothing!'

Mr Stallard took her by the shoulders. 'You must never believe that. Our marriage means everything.' He looked deep into her eyes to calm her. '*You* mean everything.'

Mrs Stallard stood back from her husband and straightened her skirts about her. 'Tell me of the note,' she demanded.

Archibald looked utterly vanquished. He dropped his gaze to the floor in shame. Before he had a chance to respond, however, there came another commotion at the front door. The bell rang with such an urgent tone that Bowman jumped in spite of himself. Mrs Stallard walked past him to the hall, her face streaked with tears. Bowman heard the door swing open and Graves' voice cutting through the air.

'We have her, sir!' the sergeant called. Bowman saw a sudden look of panic in Archibald's eyes and he too strode past the inspector, his fists clenched into tight balls. Bowman joined him in the hallway, only to see Isabella Stallard had descended the steps to the street. There, she joined Sergeant Graves and three or four police constables before a carriage. Between them, they held a ragged woman with flame red hair and pale, almost translucent skin. She thrashed wildly in their grasp, wailing in her anguish. 'Archie!' she screamed. 'Tell these men to get their filthy hands off me!'

Archibald swallowed hard, painfully aware that her cries were attracting the attention of his neighbours, then joined his wife on the roadside. Reaching out to calm her, he stroked her hair as he whispered. 'Be still, my love.'

'The man in the carriage is another tenant at Hope Place,' Graves explained. Bowman peered through the windows to see a burly man in shirtsleeves and a tattered scarf glaring back at him. 'He has confessed to demanding money from Mr Stallard with menaces.'

Isabella Stallard turned to her husband, her jaw slack with surprise. 'For the sum of a thousand pounds?'

Stallard nodded. 'Forgive me,' he said. 'This man threatened to expose me if I did not pay.'

'But you did not have the money,' Bowman interjected from the pavement.

'I am nought but a tutor, inspector. I could not hope to lay my hands upon such a price.'

Isabella planted her hands on her hips. 'So you threatened me with blackmail? You were willing to risk my reputation to save your own?'

'I could see no other way!' Archibald released his hold upon the red-haired woman and sank to his knees by the carriage.

'And you were the only one to have the occasion to plant the note in the book,' added Sergeant Graves, 'between the library lad delivering it and Mrs Stallard opening it.'

'Mrs Stallard?' spat Isabella. 'That name has no currency now.' She glared at the woman who struggled against the constables' clutches. 'Not now that I know it is so well used.'

With that, she turned from the street, stamped up the steps to the house and slammed the door shut behind her. Her meaning was clear. Archibald Stallard was no longer welcome.

'Bigamy is a crime, Sergeant Graves,' pronounced Bowman over a jar of porter later that evening. 'Archibald Stallard will be tried and sentenced accordingly.'

The Silver Cross was humming with activity. Harris' hands were a blur at the pumps. He had never looked happier.

'It seems no one wins, sir,' said Graves over the hubbub. 'The first Mrs Stallard finds herself in an asylum,' he avoided Bowman's eye at the mention of the word, 'the second finds her marriage annulled.'

Bowman nodded as he wiped the froth from his lip. 'Perhaps,' he agreed, 'but Isabella's offer to pay for the lady's treatment shows she is not above compassion. It is an irony that the very book in which Mr Stallard planted the note is a study in redemption. Perhaps she has taken Mr Dickens' lesson to heart.'

Graves beamed. 'I'll drink to that, sir,' he said as he downed the last of his beer. 'Now, if you'll excuse me, I am on a promise to Harris to provide some entertainment for the customers.'

Cracking his knuckles, Graves moved through the throng to the piano. A cheer went up in the saloon bar as the young sergeant threw himself upon the stool, and many a happy drinker gathered to clap him on the back

Bowman smiled at his companion. 'God bless us,' he said to no one in particular as he raised his glass to his lips. 'Every one.'

THE CHRISTMAS MURDERS

DECEMBER, 1892

A hard overnight rain had frozen hard as iron on the roads and paths. This Christmas Eve, the whole of London seemed an ice rink. Detective Inspector George Bowman gazed through the window of the two-horse brougham he had hailed on Finchley Road. The ice crunched beneath the wheels as they struggled for purchase. Pulling his scarf even tighter around his neck, Bowman marvelled at the morning sun sparkling on the frost. The skeletal London plane trees stood stark against the bluest of skies, their frozen fingers reaching to the heavens as if in search of warmth. The vagrants of St John's Wood had set a fire outside Lord's Cricket Ground, huddling together in the glow of its flames, pulling rags and blankets about themselves, their breath curling into the air. The dingy hovels of Marylebone shimmered with the tiny crystals that had formed on their windowpanes like delicate jewels.

Skidding down Park Lane, the brougham joined the throng of traffic making its way unsteadily towards the city centre. Bowman let his eyes wander over Hyde Park, its spacious grounds a field of frost. Passers by tucked their heads down into their coats and jammed their hands into their pockets, picking their way carefully across the network of paths that crossed from Lancaster Gate to Belgravia. As they rounded the corner into Grosvenor Place, Bowman saw a man slip on the ice. His arms windmilled comically in a vain attempt to regain balance, before he finally crashed to the path in a pile of flailing limbs. The inspector noticed his companion laugh and point before his legs, too, slipped away from beneath him. The result was a heap of helpless laughter as the two men struggled to regain their balance and their dignity. Bowman couldn't help but smile at their predicament and made a mental note to watch his footing when he stepped from the footplate at Scotland Yard.

His thoughts were interrupted by a sudden jolt. He reached out to steady himself as the carriage lurched to one side, accompanied by the sound of splitting wood. Looking up, he could see the driver in his box trying desperately to regain control of his horses. The carriage came, at last, to a juddering halt by the roadside and Bowman was able to peer out the door as the driver jumped from his perch. A small crowd gathered as he bent to examine the near side wheel.

'Looks like it's had it, mate,' offered a scarecrow of a man in a coat too large for him. There were murmurs of agreement.

'Don't reckon you'll be gettin' no tip today,' guffawed an old lady wrapped in a torn blanket. She stamped her feet for warmth as Bowman jumped from the carriage, reaching out instinctively to steady himself against its chassis as he landed. 'Reckon you'll be on Shanks' pony, now,' she tittered. Bowman could smell the scent of gin on her breath.

The driver had taken his hat from his head to mop at his brow. 'We must have hit a rut,' he growled as the horses shifted impatiently in their harnesses.

Bowman looked out into the road. Churned up by the rain, it had frozen overnight into solid rifts and valleys of ice and mud. It looked hard as stone.

Bowman slipped a handful of change from his pocket and thanked the driver for his service. The poor man nodded back by way of thanks, then kicked his wheel in anger.

'All right, mate, we'll soon have yer right,' said the scarecrow. 'Don't yer carry a spare?'

Bowman turned his face to the biting wind and picked his way carefully down Piccadilly. Despite the conditions, London was waking all around him. The smarter stores had already succumbed to the demands of the season, proudly displaying the Christmas trees that had become more ubiquitous in recent years. Candles burned in shop windows, lending an enticing glow to their wares. The finest jewellers and milliners kept awkward company with butchers and chop houses, the latter firing up their ovens for the morning trade. Bowman was met with the heady aroma of spices and roasting meat as he turned onto Trafalgar Square. His toes were numb from the cold.

On the corner with Whitehall, Bowman almost fell over a man at the kerbside. As he made his apologies, he saw the man was distracted by something over the inspector's shoulder.

'Spare an ha'penny for an old soldier, guvnor?' the man said, suddenly, before Bowman had a chance to see what had caught his attention. His filthy face was lean and haggard. One eye was missing or damaged behind sunken lids, whilst the other blinked against the cold. Bowman could only guess at how the man had come by such an appalling injury.

'Left it in Majuba,' the man explained, tapping at his sunken eye socket. The inspector raised an eyebrow as he dug deep into his pockets.

'Africa?' he breathed, his voice hoarse. He had heard of it, and of the defeat of the British army at the hands of the Boers.

The man nodded. 'Fifty Eighth Regiment. The Northamptonshires.' His voice quivered with pride as he spoke. 'Fine bunch of lads. Shame they don't look after their own when the fighting's done.'

As Bowman wrestled with his change, his attention, too, was drawn across the road to Spring Gardens. There, a familiar silhouette was bent in urgent conversation with a stout man in a ridiculously tall stovepipe hat. The silhouette belonged to Harris, the landlord of The Silver Cross on Whitehall. All he could see of the other man was a pair of great white mutton chop sideburns. It was impossible to discern their words at this distance, but they were clearly agitated. First one then the other would jab at the air with his fingers as he spoke. Periodically,

Bowman noticed a hand go to a face or bunching into a fist. They were clearly doing more than exchanging pleasantries.

'They picked us off one by one from the long grass,' the soldier was continuing, as if to distract Bowman from the sight of the two men arguing. 'Lesser men panicked and fled.' He gave a bitter cackle. 'Guess those who ran away are tucked up somewhere safe now, while those who stood their ground have been left to rot.'

The inspector nodded absently as he flicked the man a ha'penny.

'God bless you, sir,' the soldier rasped. 'And a Merry Christmas to you.'

Bowman's attention drifted across the road again. Their argument at an end, the two men were going their separate ways along Spring Gardens; Harris back to The Silver Cross, the stout man in the stovepipe hat across Trafalgar Square to the church at St Martin-In-The-Fields.

'Yes, quite,' Bowman stuttered, absently. 'Merry Christmas.'

The inspector shook his head. His ears felt frozen. Straightening his coat about him, he turned carefully down Whitehall on his way to Scotland Yard, pausing only to peer in through the windows of The Silver Cross where Harris was busy preparing the bar for the morning trade.

The view from Bowman's office had never looked prettier. A blanket of frost had been laid across the rooftops and the air was as clear as he could remember. The proliferation of tanneries, breweries and even less savoury industries often lent the capital's air a sickly pallor and it was a rare day indeed when quite so much was visible from his window. Beneath him, rolled the Thames. The artery of London, carrying its lifeblood from its upper reaches to the estuary and beyond, the River Thames was a conveyor of trade and, Bowman knew, crime. The market in stolen goods depended upon its tributaries and tides. An entire industry of crime was predicated upon its ebb and flow. Sergeant Graves stood at the desk behind the inspector with the results of one such example.

'Inspector Crouch has broken a smuggling ring in a warehouse near Tilbury,' he was enthusing, his eyes bright. 'Local officials reported their suspicions that it contained more than tea.'

Bowman turned from the window, his interest piqued.

'Crouch inspected the dock master's records and discovered the arrival of a small boat was logged twice a day at the same time.'

Bowman frowned. 'I do not see the significance.'

Graves leaned over the desk in his excitement. 'Tilbury is tidal. And the tide shifts throughout the month. According to the master's logs, that boat would have been docking at times when the tide was too low to berth.'

Bowman nodded. 'A mistake, certainly,'

'Indeed. And that was enough. The false records concealed an opium smuggling operation at the docks. Upon raiding the warehouse, Crouch discovered that it did, indeed, hold more than tea,'

Bowman let the air whistle between his teeth. Opium was perfectly legal in various preparations but there was a thriving black market for its purest form.

'Inspector Crouch has been busy enough for us all,' Bowman smiled.

The two men were interrupted by a knock at the door.

'Come!' Bowman barked as he sat at his desk. For a moment, he half expected Inspector Hicks to come blundering in. Instead, he was greeted by the sight of a young sergeant with a fresh face and pomaded hair. The buttons on his uniform shone in the light from Bowman's window.

'We've got a body off St Martin's Lane,' panted Sergeant Matthews. 'Found by a boy this morning in a yard near the printing works.'

He moved to the map that spanned almost the entire width of Bowman's office wall. Lifting a finger, he tapped at the location of an alley opposite the Trafalgar Square Theatre. 'Knife to the throat.'

Bowman frowned. He was not looking forward to going back out into the cold.

'Shall we, sir?' True to form, Graves was already bounding to the door like a puppy. Not for the first time, Bowman envied him his energy.

As the two detectives strode up Whitehall, they had to fight to maintain their footing. Though bright, the morning sun had still not reached the height of its powers, and the icy pavements remained treacherous. All around them, passers by clutched at lampposts or groped at walls for support. The urchins that were wont to run between the legs of the shoppers now slid in the road, their arms outstretched. Their laughter echoed off the buildings around them, competing with the crackle of ice beneath the wheels of the passing carriages. A man selling chestnuts from a glowing brazier on the corner with Trafalgar Square smiled at the queue before him. Men and women from all stations of life stood shoulder to shoulder and exchanged pleasantries as they waited patiently in line, their faces flushed with cold.

As Bowman and Graves rounded the corner onto St Martin's Lane, they could already see the commotion. A few hundred yards ahead, a crowd had gathered by the entrance to an alleyway. Two uniformed constables stood with their arms crossed, barring the way. As the two detectives approached, they turned as one.

'Sorry, mate,' barked one, 'you ain't goin' down there.'

Bowman fumbled for his papers in an inside pocket, resenting the fact that he had to undo the buttons to do so. 'Detective Inspector Bowman,' he said as he handed the paper over. 'This is Sergeant Graves.'

'Beggin' your pardon, sir,' smiled the other as he peered over his companion's shoulder to read. 'Got a lot of gawpers today.'

He gestured to the motley ensemble of onlookers that, even now, was growing apace.

'Scotland Yard!' crowed a young lady with a basket of fruit. Clearly taking a fancy to Bowman's companion, she sidled up to Sergeant Graves. 'Arrest me now, sergeant,' she said with a wink. 'Lock me up and do what you will.' There was a peel of laughter from the crowd and Bowman noticed much nudging of elbows.

Graves couldn't help but smile. 'Got to be found guilty of something first, I'm afraid,' he sparkled.

'Oh, I'm guilty of plenty, dearie,' the young woman announced, bumping him with her hip.

'Come on, Rosie,' came another voice from the crowd. 'Let's go and try at Covent Garden.'

With a wink, Rosie turned away to ply her trade with her partner, another young woman with a tray of bread.

Bowman shook his head as Sergeant Graves chuckled amiably, his blond curls dancing about his head. Bowman had never understood how, firstly, Graves could maintain such levity in the face of so grim an investigation and, secondly, how he could forego a hat on such a cold day.

'That's quite all right,' Bowman sighed as he took his paper back from the constable. 'You're doing sterling work. Any idea who the man is?'

'The boy that found him says his name is Nathaniel

Spendlove. He's landlord of The Salisbury Stores, across the way there. The lad says he'd run errands for the man, so he's certain.'

The constable nodded across the road to the public house that stood on the corner of St Martin's Court. The Salisbury Stores was a newer public house than many. Even from this distance, Bowman could see its paintwork and signage gleaming in the morning sun.

With a tip of his hat, the inspector shouldered his way past the constables, Sergeant Graves following in his wake.

The alley was covered for part of the way, but soon opened up to the elements. It seemed colder still here and Bowman plunged his hands into his coat pockets. The sheer walls around him deprived the passageway of any light and so the frost was harder still. Even so, Bowman could see it had recently been disturbed. A pair of footprints led the way to the furthest reaches of the alley, where it narrowed to a flight of steps. There, laying at a seemingly impossible angle, was a body. As the two men approached, they could see the ice around it was thick with blood. Bowman could see it had also spattered up the walls. The man lay face down in the dirt, his arms and legs twisted into alarming shapes. It must have been a frenzied death, Bowman thought. Desperate.

'Not too pretty, is it, sir?' whistled Graves, already squatting on his haunches to examine the body further. 'Looks like a knife, for sure,' he continued as he rolled the poor man over. 'Just as Matthews said.'

Bowman nodded. The man's clothes were stained a deep red. A deep gash gaped at his neck. Bowman bent to look closer at the wretch's face. There was something familiar about his white mutton chops, discoloured though they now were with the man's blood. He cast his eyes about the alley in search of confirmation. Sure enough, there by the side of the steps, lay a battered stovepipe hat.

'I know this man, Graves.'

Sergeant Graves looked up, alarmed. 'Sir?'

'Or rather, I saw him.' Bowman's moustache was twitching. 'This morning, talking with Harris on Spring Gardens.'

'Harris? From The Silver Cross?'

Bowman nodded. 'The very same. It was a most animated conversation, then the man walked to St Martin-In-The-Fields.' The inspector rose as he thought. 'And now he is dead.'

'If Spendlove was the landlord of The Salisbury Stores, I shouldn't be at all surprised if he was known to Harris. There's but half a mile between them.'

Bowman had taken several steps back to the mouth of the alley. 'He's but recently dead,' mused Bowman, aloud. 'Perhaps within the last half an hour. There must surely have been witnesses to his being dragged off the street.'

'Doubt it, sir.' Graves rose to join him, looking out to the street beyond. 'Look at them.'

Bowman followed Graves' gaze. The two constables had done a fine job of dispersing the crowd, and the view was clear. Almost to a man, the passers by that processed carefully along the pavements did so with their heads down.

'They wouldn't notice if the Ghost of Christmas Past himself appeared before them,' Graves beamed.

Bowman stamped his feet against the cold. 'Graves, I want you to go to The Salisbury Stores to learn what you can of Spendlove. I'll go to Harris to see what he has to say for himself. There is nothing more to be learned here.'

'Oh, I don't know, sir,' said Graves, beckoning his superior to join him. 'What are we to make of this?'

As Bowman squatted beside him, the young sergeant reached out to Spendlove's hand. It was bunched into a fist as if holding tight onto something. Uncurling the dead man's fingers, Graves opened his palm to reveal several waxy leaves sticking to the man's skin. Bowman's eyebrows rose as Graves turned to face him. 'It's holly, sir,' he said, perplexed.

The two men walked from the alley, each in thought. 'Have the body taken to Doctor John Crane at Charing Cross Hospital,' Bowman barked to the two constables on guard. 'He'll know what to do if he discovers anything out of the ordinary.' The constables nodded curtly, then argued amongst themselves as to who should walk to the nearest police station in search of a Black Mariah.

As he opened the door to The Silver Cross, Bowman was dismayed to see his favourite chair by the fire was already occupied. A fat man in an ankle-length coat was sprawled across it, a newspaper upon his lap. With the morning progressing, it seemed many people had simply decided to take their midday meal a little earlier. Bowman noticed a pot of stew bubbling gamely in the small kitchen beyond the bar. As he moved through the throng, he could see Harris toiling with a ladle to fulfil another order.

'Make way for Scotland Yard!'

The shout came from a small man at the bar and resulted in the turning of several heads. The man was blessed with a halo of bright red hair and a mouthful of haphazard teeth.

'All right, Mayberry,' Harris called from the little kitchen. 'If the whole of Scotland Yard withdrew their custom, I'd have no custom left.'

Though his manner was jovial enough, Bowman detected a touch of frost in Harris' response.

'Don't worry, inspector,' Mayberry purred. 'I have known Harris for many years. He has spoken of you often.' The little man smiled, reaching for a pipe from his pocket. Bowman noticed the gaps in his teeth resulted in a strange whistling sound as he breathed.

'Indeed?' the inspector replied, warily.

'Only to say how much I value your custom, inspector,' chimed Harris from the stewpot, clearly uncomfortable at the turn in the conversation. 'And that of your colleagues.'

'You're the fellow that was in the madhouse,' the man leered as he struck a match against the bar. There was a sudden silence in the room. Bowman felt all eyes upon him. He swallowed.

'Wish you were better at holding your tongue than you are at holding your beer, Mayberry,' hissed Harris guiltily as he tried to avoid the inspector's eye.

'If the beer was better, you might not have to rely on madmen for custom.' Mayberry cackled to himself, pleased with his response.

Bowman blinked as Harris brushed past with his bowl of stew and made his way to a table in the saloon. Sliding it across to a man who sat waiting with a handkerchief tucked into his collar, Harris called over his shoulder, desperate to lighten the atmosphere. 'Your first drink'll be on the house, Inspector Bowman.'

Mayberry puffed on his pipe, sending clouds of blue smoke into the air around him. Bowman eyed the man carefully as Harris made his way back to the bar. He held his head low so that his lank hair hung across his eyes, the better to avoid Bowman's gaze.

'Mayberry is a civil servant in Whitehall,' explained Harris at the pump.

Bowman nodded.

'Colonial Office. He thinks that means he can lord it over the rest of us.' Harris flashed Bowman a conciliatory smile as he passed over a pint of porter.

'I am merely a cog in the machine of government.' Mayberry raised a glass to his lips. 'But I like to think I provide a little lubrication.' He drank deep, slamming his glass on the bar as he finished.

Bowman noticed the hubbub had returned to the room. Looking around, he saw heads bent in conversation again. The moment had passed.

'Harris, I need to speak with you.' The inspector leaned over the bar. 'Might we find a quiet corner?'

Harris nodded, certain he was about to experience the detective's wrath. 'Follow me into the back room,' he said at last, lifting the flap in the counter so that Bowman might follow.

Sergeant Graves had interrupted Mrs Spendlove at her housework. He had been directed to her home off Tottenham Court Road by a surly barman at The Salisbury Stores.

Irene Spendlove was a sturdy woman with an apron tied round her waist and her hair tied into a bun. She had been cleaning cutlery when Graves knocked at the door. The sergeant found her sweating over a canteen of knives.

'I take in work where I can,' she had explained. 'These are for Mr and Mrs Levitt in Knightsbridge.' Graves had to profess that he had not heard of them.

Now, he stood in the parlour of the small but smart house on Chenies Street, his heart thumping in his chest. He had not considered that Mrs Spendlove might not yet know of her husband's death.

'Mrs Spendlove,' he began, 'I am here on a most serious matter.'

Irene twisted her apron in her fingers, suddenly fearful.

'Oh lord,' she gasped. 'Is it Nathaniel?'

Graves nodded, sadly. 'I'm afraid I must tell you that he is dead.'

Mrs Spendlove's hands went instinctively to her mouth. 'An

accident?' She whispered.

'Worse.' Graves struggled to find the right words. 'Won't you sit?' He gestured to a small chair by the window. Irene complied, her eyes brimming with tears.

'What has happened?' she asked, her voice cracking with emotion.

Graves took a breath. 'Mrs Spendlove, your husband's body was found in an alleyway off St Martin's Lane this morning.'

Irene fumbled in an apron pocket for a handkerchief.

'I have just come from the scene of the crime.'

The poor woman's eyes grew wide in astonishment. 'Crime?' she echoed.

Graves cleared his throat and watched Mrs Spendlove carefully as he continued. 'Your husband was murdered,' he said, simply.

'Murdered?' Mrs Spendlove pronounced the word as if it were something entirely alien to her. 'But... *how*?'

Graves lowered himself into the chair opposite her, suddenly conscious of the paper ornaments that adorned the mantelpiece. They had been cut into the shape of snowflakes and Christmas trees. He leaned forward over his knees as he explained.

'It seems he was killed with a knife to the throat.'

Mrs Spendlove threw her hands to her face. 'What shall I tell the children? And at Christmas, too?'

Graves' heart stopped. 'You have children?'

He looked again at the paper ornaments and saw that they had clearly been made by small hands.

Mrs Spendlove nodded through her tears. 'They are both at school for the morning. What will I tell them?'

Graves had no answer for her. 'I am sorry,' he whispered. 'Mrs Spendlove, I must ask. Is there anyone who would wish your husband dead?'

Irene gave a dry laugh in spite of her grief. 'He is a pub

landlord. What do you think?'

Graves blinked.

'I am sorry, Sergeant Graves. This is all so terrible and I am afraid I am quite at sea.'

Graves met her eyes. 'Did Mr Spendlove show any change in his behaviour over recent weeks? Did he, for example, have any money worries?'

Mrs Spendlove drew a breath, baulking at the personal nature of Graves' questions.

'Mrs Spendlove,' the sergeant entreated, 'is there anything that would shed more light on your husband's death?'

Irene Spendlove seemed to steel herself. 'I can think of nothing,' she said at last.

Graves could not help but admit he was disappointed.

'I am sorry, Sergeant Graves,' Irene continued, 'but we have lived a model life together. Nathaniel was a perfect husband to me and a perfect father to our poor children.' She dabbed at her eyes. 'He moved us out of The Salisbury Stores when the little ones came along, determined they should not have to grow up in a public house.' There was a look of pride in her eyes. 'He has been determined to make a success of himself since leaving the railways. The Salisbury Stores gave him the means to do so.'

Graves thought. 'Then he has done well at The Salisbury?'

Mrs Spendlove smoothed her apron across her lap, absently, as she spoke. 'Nathaniel was its second landlord, but it was his third public house. He went to much trouble to make it a place worth spending time in, and fought hard to attract the right sort of person.'

If Graves detected a hint of snobbery in her response, he did not let it show.

'Where is he now, Sergeant Graves?' Irene had risen to stand at the fireplace, her back to the room.

'His body is at Charing Cross Hospital.'

'I suppose you will need an identification of the body. Might I see him?'

'I shall make the necessary arrangements,' Graves replied as he stood. 'And I will be sure a cab is here to take you. The paths are treacherous.'

Irene Spendlove turned to face him. 'Thank you, Sergeant Graves,' she said quietly. Then, with more force, she leaned towards him. 'I want you to find the monster who killed my husband. And I want you to string him up.' For a moment, her whole body trembled. Then, with a breath, Mrs Spendlove composed herself again. 'You will see your own way out?'

Graves dipped his head. 'Of course,' he said. As he moved to the door, he took a final look at the widow by the fire. He noticed her hand move to the mantelpiece as one by one, she removed each of the paper Christmas decorations and threw them into the fire.

'The poor man,' Harris sighed as he flicked his long hair from his eyes. 'But, inspector, what has this got to do with me?'

Bowman leaned back against the table in the small back room. Even here, there was a tang of tobacco and alcohol in the air. He could hear the hum of the saloon bar through the walls. The room was small and packed with boxes. A few pieces of broken furniture stood at alarming angles. A tattered rag hung at the window in place of a curtain. Far from the fire by the bar, Bowman felt there was a chill in the very walls. He could see his breath as he spoke.

'Harris, I think you might know the man.'

Harris' leathery face creased into an expression of concern. 'Know him?' he gasped.

'It was Nathaniel Spendlove.' Bowman noticed a flash of

alarm in Harris' eyes. "I believe he was the landlord at The Salisbury Stores on St Martin's Lane. He was found in an alleyway just opposite.'

Harris rubbed his jaw as if in thought. Bowman thought the gesture just a little too theatrical.

'I knew *of* him, certainly,' the landlord admitted, slowly. 'But I can't say I knew him well.'

Bowman sighed, his moustache twitching. 'Then how can you explain the fact that I saw you conversing with him on Spring Gardens only this morning?'

Harris seemed surprised by the revelation, but did his best to hide it. At first he feigned a cough, then puffed and harrumphed as he sought for an answer. 'He took me quite by surprise,' he said, at last.

Bowman raised his eyebrows.

'At first, I thought he was accosting me, such was his vehemence.' Harris was thinking fast. 'Turns out The Salisbury Stores is in trouble. Losing money hand over fist.' He swallowed before continuing. 'To put it plainly, Inspector Bowman, he was after money.'

Bowman narrowed his eyes. That would certainly explain the animated nature of the discussion he had witnessed that morning. 'Money?'

'He was an inveterate gambler. I dare say he'd lost the proceeds from the Salisbury on a bad wager.'

The inspector frowned. 'You said you did not know him well.'

There was a pause before Harris tapped his nose. 'Word on the street, inspector. Word on the street.'

'And would the word on the street extend to knowing just who might have killed him?'

Harris shook his head. 'That I couldn't tell you.'

Bowman was certain the landlord was hiding something. 'Harris,' he began, 'can you see why I might have an interest in your encounter with Spendlove given that, just an hour later, I found myself kneeling over his body?'

Harris nodded, weakly. 'I can certainly see how that might look, yes.'

Bowman let the moment hang in the air. 'I will leave it there for now,' he said, at last, 'but I might have more questions for you at Scotland Yard.'

Harris' jaw hung slack for a second. 'Of course,' he nodded.

'There is one other thing, a detail that has me perplexed.'

Harris swallowed. 'Oh?'

Bowman spoke slowly, keen to watch the landlord's reaction. 'A single sprig of holly was found in Spendlove's hand.' He held Harris in his gaze. 'I am at a loss as to its significance.'

Harris' hair fell into his eyes as he shook his head. 'I can't think what it might mean, sir.' Harris licked his lips as if they were suddenly dry. 'Perhaps it has no significance, at all.'

Bowman eased himself from the table and pulled his coat about him as if to signify the end of the conversation.

'Inspector,' Harris said suddenly as Bowman reached for the door. 'I am sorry for Mayberry. He has ever had a loose tongue.'

Bowman nodded, remembering Mayberry's jibes about the lunatic asylum. He could only have known through Harris. 'Then it seems he is not alone.'

Harris dropped his gaze to the floor.

'I will avail myself of your stew, Harris,' Bowman announced, finally, 'and then I must continue my investigations into the death of Nathaniel Spendlove.'

Emerging back into the bar, Bowman was relieved to see the crowd had thinned. He smiled to himself as he noticed his favourite chair by the fire was available and, having hung his coat on a hook by the chimney breast, he sat back to wait for

Sergeant Graves.

He appeared at last as Bowman ate the last of his stew.

'I had not thought to ruin someone's Christmas when I woke up this morning,' the sergeant sighed as he slumped into the chair opposite.

Bowman dabbed at the corners of his mouth with a napkin. 'I am sorry, Graves,' he said with feeling. It was always a disconcerting sight to see Graves brought low.

The young sergeant ran his fingers through his curls. 'He was a father, too.' He puffed out his cheeks. 'I do not know how Mrs Spendlove will cope.' As he leaned back in his chair, he told Bowman of his visit to Chenies Street and the sad picture Mrs Spendlove had presented.

Bowman nodded in sympathy. 'It's a sorry tale, indeed, Graves,' he said as he stared into the flames of the fire.

Sergeant Graves shook his head, as if to rid himself of his despondency. 'What did Harris have to say for himself?'

Bowman turned to the bar to seek out the landlord. Harris, he noticed, was trying his best to keep out of sight. 'He was hiding something, Graves. Though heaven alone knows what.' He turned to his companion. 'He suggested Spendlove had money problems and that was the subject of their altercation this morning. Was there any hint of that in your interview with his wife?'

Graves shook his head. 'Quite the reverse,' he admitted. 'Mrs Spendlove presented him as nothing less than a model husband, intent on providing for his family. Their rooms looked comfortable enough.'

'Then why would Harris impugn Spendlove's character in such a manner?' Bowman looked back at the bar as Harris disappeared into the back room.

'Maybe we don't know Harris at all,' whispered Graves as he

followed his superior's gaze.

'Maybe not,' conceded Bowman. 'But perhaps there's someone who does.'

In stark contrast to the year before, Christmas Day was spent alone. In truth, Bowman was grateful for it. He attended Eucharist on Christmas morning, but stood at the back of the church so as not to catch anyone's eye. Though not especially religious, Bowman had felt a need to hear the expressions of hope and joy contained within the sacrament.

His landlady brought down some goose for dinner after which he walked on Hampstead Heath. He stopped by the ponds to watch a young family attempt to launch a kite into the still, lazy air, impressed at their persistence. As he strolled to higher ground, Bowman let his eyes wander across the horizon. To the north, he knew, lay Colney Hatch. He could not help but think of the poor wretches who languished there. Perhaps a good many of them might never leave. He thought of Wilkes and Taylor, of the matron and the chaplain. Most of all, he thought of the strange alienist whose methods had led to Bowman's recovery. He could not pretend to understand them fully, but he was grateful to feel, at last, as though he was something of the man he had been before he had lost his wife. He was able to think of her now with none of the anguish that had so plagued him before his treatment. He could even view his part in her death as if from a distance, dispassionately. Of course, he wished she were with him - and could even imagine it being so - but he no longer succumbed to the delusions that had plagued him. He could see, now, that her frequent appearances before him since her death had been the work of a feverish mind. He could even start to imagine a future without her. He flinched at the thought almost guiltily, then turned towards the path that would lead him home. As he reached the viaduct, his thoughts turned to Harris and his part in Spendlove's death. Something Graves had said at The Silver Cross had bothered him. 'Maybe we don't know Harris at all,' Graves had suggested, and perhaps he was right. Harris had felt like a constant in Bowman's experiences as a detective; dependable and unchanging. To consider that he might have something to do with Spendlove's murder troubled the detective inspector enormously. But why else would he have prevaricated so? He had been evasive at best, and Bowman dreaded the reason why.

As he tripped down the steps to his basement rooms on Belsize Crescent, Bowman cursed the fact that he could not further pursue his enquiries for another two days.

Boxing Day passed in equal quietude. As he tidied his rooms, Bowman realised he was getting used to being alone. He decided to spend the afternoon rearranging his furniture, an activity which led to him discarding the things he would no longer need. Aside from a picture of Anna, he determined that he would be rid of everything of hers that would not be of use. Unsure what to do with her clothing, he bundled it up and carried it upstairs to his surprised landlady. She stood, at first, with her arms folded across her bosom, a suspicious look upon her face. At last, she accepted the gift, perhaps relieved that she would no longer have to step carefully around the clothes on Bowman's floor as she cleaned. As there was still time in the day, she resolved to box them up, as was the tradition, and leave them at the church for distribution to the poor. It was a gesture that Bowman had not thought of but one of which, he knew, Anna would have approved.

Finally, the festivities were over. Bowman felt relieved that he had navigated his way through Christmas so artfully. He was dismayed, however, to find a dusting of snow had been laid down overnight. He trudged miserably to Finchley Road to find a cab, then sat in contemplative silence on his way to Whitehall.

At last, the Colonial Office rose above him. Stepping carefully from the footplate, Bowman paused to look up at the building before him. Towering over five stories, it was faced with Portland stone, giving the whole construction a solidity quite befitting an office of state. An impressive entrance stood beneath a weighty portico supported on three arches and it was towards the centre of these that Bowman turned his feet.

Pushing at the heavy wooden door, he found himself inside an opulent entrance hall. Large portraits and accompanying coats of arms hung from the walls, their subjects staring solemnly down from beneath powdered wigs. Bowman had no doubt but that they had been powerful men in their time and had been afforded their lofty positions accordingly. Even in death, they stood in judgement over the comings and goings of the Empire.

The inspector's footsteps echoed to the vaulted ceiling as he paced to a large desk set in a corner. A few men stood about, some in formal dress, others in uniform. Bowman felt suddenly very conspicuous. Just as he was about to approach the rather po-faced man behind the desk, he heard his name echoing from the wide staircase to his left hand side.

'Inspector Bowman, I do declare!'

Bowman swept his hat from his head and knocked the melted frost from its brim. 'Mr Mayberry,' he smiled with some effort, 'you have saved me from enquiring after your whereabouts.'

Mayberry was descending the marble stairs beside a tall man in a Fez.

'Indeed?' Mayberry's eyebrows rose in mock concern as he approached. 'Am I to be *investigated*?'

Bowman was suddenly aware that he was the centre of attention. A large man in a corner lowered his newspaper to watch. Two men in colourful African dress leaned from behind a pillar, the better to follow proceedings.

'Inspector Bowman, might I introduce you to the Ambassador Of The Ottoman Empire?'

The man beside him flashed a tense smile beneath a wide moustache and bowed his head in greeting.

'The pleasure is all mine,' he said in an exotically accented English. For all his manners, he looked eager to leave and be about his day.

Bowman nodded his head in response, unsure how to address an ambassador. He could sense Mayberry stifling a laugh at his expense.

'That was a most productive meeting, Your Excellency,' said Mayberry easily. 'I shall look forward to many such more. Do let me know if there is anything I can do to improve your stay.'

The ambassador nodded towards the tall windows that looked out into the street beyond. 'Perhaps you might do something about the weather?' he teased. Bowman sensed it was more than a joke.

Mayberry gave a polite laugh. 'I'm afraid, ambassador, that that is beyond even my powers.' Bowman noticed how relaxed the little man was in such exalted company. In truth, he envied him for it. 'Do send my regards to your wife,' Mayberry continued.

The ambassador reached forward to shake the civil servant by the hand, then made his way smartly to the desk to retrieve his coat.

Bowman looked at Mayberry through narrowed eyes. He was struck by how different this version of the man was from that he had seen in The Silver Cross. Where the one had been crass and insulting, this one seemed the very epitome of manners. Perhaps Harris had been right to insulate he could not hold his drink.

'How may I be of assistance, Detective Inspector Bowman?'

smiled the man before him, his red hair glinting in the light.

Bowman looked around him. 'Is there somewhere we may talk in private?'

Mayberry smiled again, evidently pleased at the opportunity to play the host.

'Of course, inspector. Won't you follow me?'

As he turned back to the staircase, he launched into an excited monologue concerning the building around him. 'The architect was most unhappy with the finished building, you know. Lord Palmerston rejected his original proposal and so he was forced, quite literally, back to the drawing board.' Mayberry chuckled as they ascended the stairs. 'I find the classical style to be rather fitting. It serves to impress upon our visitors the permanence of the Empire.'

Mayberry waved the inspector into a smart office with wood panelling on the walls. An impressive desk took up most of the room, laden with books. A globe stood on a shelf by the window. A wing-backed chair was the only other furniture.

'It is a humble office, but mine own,' grinned Mayberry as he threw himself onto his chair. Bowman guessed the lack of additional seating was deliberate. No wonder the Ottoman Ambassador had been so eager to leave.

Mayberry reached for a pipe and leaned back. 'I have just fifteen minutes until I am due to meet with the Under Secretary,' he announced. 'I trust you can say all you need to say in a quarter of an hour?'

'If you are forthcoming I may be gone in less,' Bowman snapped back. 'I need to talk with you about Harris.'

Mayberry raised his eyebrows as he bit down on the stem of his pipe. 'Emmett Harris? At The Silver Cross?'

Bowman nodded. He had not heard Harris' Christian name before. In fact, he had never considered that he might even *have* a Christian name. 'I understand you know him of old.'

Mayberry blew smoke from between his clenched teeth. Bowman was alarmed to see the bit of his pipe was clamped into a gap between them. 'I've known him since his railway days.'

Bowman frowned. 'He worked on the railways?'

'For a time,' nodded Mayberry, amused that Bowman could take an interest in such things. 'I got out before he did, mind. Found meself a job in government.'

'Where?' Bowman shifted on his feet.

'York, at first, for the Board Of Trade.' He had affected an airy nonchalance. 'Then, some seven months ago, I was offered a position here.' He leaned over his huge desk. 'A position I find to be most favourable.' Mayberry let go great clouds of smoke as he chuckled. 'That was when I decided to look up old Emmett. I had heard he had a public house nearby, and so I found him at The Silver Cross.'

Bowman gnawed at his lip. 'What was Harris' position in the railway?'

Mayberry laughed. 'Drunk on his back, for the most part. Although, in truth, he earned it by day.'

'He was a navvy?' Bowman's eyes narrowed. He knew the work of the railway gangs to be hard and dangerous. The navvies would move as they laid their track, erecting makeshift turf and timber shacks on the embankments in which to live. They would spend their days digging, carrying and laying explosives and their nights drinking and fighting. With his wiry frame, Harris seemed a world away from the type of man who lived such a life. He was struck again by how little he knew of the landlord's past. Harris had certainly never volunteered any facts about his younger days but then, supposed Bowman, he had never asked.

'It was a brutal life, Inspector Bowman.' Mayberry patted his desk. 'You may imagine how keen I was to leave my shovel behind for the life of an office worker.'

Bowman understood entirely. Mayberry had done well for himself. 'And Harris?'

Mayberry rose from his chair and walked to gaze out the window. A bank of grey clouds threatened more snow. 'Harris continued for some months. As I understand it, an incident necessitated him leaving some time later.'

Bowman's moustache twitched. 'Incident?' he echoed.

'In the Copenhagen Tunnel. I do not know the details,' Mayberry admitted, his back to the room. 'But it was enough to see Harris and some others out of a job.'

'And he has never spoken to you of it?'

Mayberry turned to face Bowman and ran a hand through his hair. 'He is a closed book, inspector.'

Bowman thought back to his interview with Harris at The Silver Cross. A closed book he was, indeed.

'Where might I learn more of this incident?'

Mayberry smiled a crooked smile and rubbed his chin. 'Not here at the Commonwealth Office, that is for sure.'

Bowman was downcast. 'Then you can be of no further assistance?'

Mayberry spread his hands wide as if to show he had no more to give.

'Mr Mayberry,' Bowman began, 'you should know I am investigating a murder.'

Mayberry's eyes grew wide. 'And you suspect Emmett Harris?'

'I did not say as much.'

Mayberry was agog. 'But why else would you ask so many questions? I had never considered Harris a murderer.'

'He was never violent as a navvy?'

'No more than any other,' mused Mayberry. 'And certainly

not of a disposition to kill.'

Bowman nodded. He was sure the man was right, but then…

He took a breath. 'Thank you, Mr Mayberry.'

'I can only apologise for not being of more assistance.' The little man with the red hair moved to see Bowman out. 'But perhaps you could enquire at the Great Northern Railway offices in King's Cross? Their records might shed a little more light on the matter.'

'A navvy?' Detective Sergeant Anthony Graves was intrigued. 'Harris?

The inspector had called in on Scotland Yard following his meeting in Whitehall. There, he had convinced Sergeant Graves to accompany him to King's Cross. In truth, the sergeant had needed no convincing at all. After exchanging the compliments of the season and enquiring how Bowman had spent his Christmas Day, Graves had shrugged on his coat, eager to be about the investigation.

'According to certain information I have come by,' Bowman confirmed, 'he lived an itinerant life in his younger days.'

Graves gave a whistle. 'I always considered him a dark horse.' He seemed almost in awe of the man.

'He was involved in some incident or other that saw him dismissed from his employment. But where does Spendlove fit into all this?' Bowman sighed. 'And the sprig of holly?'

'I don't know about the holly,' Graves replied, 'but there might be a connection to Spendlove.'

Bowman turned to his companion, his eyes watering in the bitter chill of the air. 'How so?'

Graves leaned towards the inspector, conspiratorially. 'Mrs Spendlove said something about her husband working on the railways prior to becoming a landlord.'

Bowman frowned. 'It seems a path well-trod.'

'Could it just be a coincidence?'

'I don't know, Graves. But I do know that Harris is holding something back, and perhaps the answer lies behind those doors.' Bowman gestured to the offices of The Great Northern Railway that stood across the road.

King's Cross Station stood, dirty, in the snow. In the forty years since it had been built, it had outgrown itself as a small child outgrows an overcoat. It had been built and opened as a terminus to the East Coast Mainline but, over the successive years, had grown to accommodate the various suburban lines that, along with the River Thames, were the capital's lifeblood. Its original two platforms, one for arrival and one for departure, had been added to and added to again so that it was now a web of iron and steel united only by a single footbridge that connected each platform. As the two detectives watched their cab slide away on the icy road, they were suddenly engulfed by a tide of people, all flowing from the station behind them.

'Come on Graves,' called Bowman and, together, they carefully navigated the Euston Road to enter the building opposite.

The offices of The Great Northern Railway were functional, at best. A large door gave onto a cavernous but plain hall lined with tiles. Bare electric bulbs hung from the ceiling, lending the place a sterile air. Bowman was reminded of a hospital or even, and he shuddered at the thought, Colney Hatch.

A line of bored people, mostly men in long coats and top hats, waited in a queue for a teller's window. A few others sat on low wooden benches beneath windows. What they were waiting for, Bowman could only guess.

'Reckon he's our man?' Graves nodded over to where a portly man stood in the uniform of The Great Northern Railway, a corduroy hat jammed on his head. He chewed the damp stump of a cigarette as he surveyed the scene before him.

As Bowman and Graves strode across the concourse towards him, the man clearly chose to pretend that he had not seen them.

'Good morning,' chimed Graves, mischievously.

The man snapped open his pocket watch, as if to be certain. 'It is,' he relented, at last. 'Just.'

'We are from Scotland Yard,' Graves proclaimed.

'Oh, yes? And I'm a monkey's uncle.' The portly man spat the end of this cigarette to the floor and ground it underfoot as he spoke.

'That's as maybe,' retorted Bowman, impatiently, 'but we are in need of information.'

The man had yet to make eye contact. 'Concerning what?'

Graves stepped forward and offered him a smile. 'Something called the Copenhagen Tunnel.'

The man sighed. 'What of it?'

'We need to see records of its construction,' Bowman interjected. 'Are they held here?'

'I dare say.' The man had reached into his pocket to retrieve a pouch of tobacco.

Bowman unfolded his identification papers. 'Then I dare say there'd be no need to charge you with the obstruction of an investigation.'

At last, the man deigned to look at the detective inspector. Rolling his eyes, he shook his head. 'Name's Giddings,' he rasped. 'I'd be grateful if you could remember it when it comes to recording how helpful I've been.'

Graves could barely contain himself. Sharing a look, the two detectives followed the reluctant Giddings to a door in the corner by the teller's window.

'I'll be five minutes, Dawes,' Giddings announced as he reached for a ring of keys at his belt. 'Scotland Yard are after me.' He gestured with his thumb at the two men behind him.

'Right you are,' Dawes replied, cheerily. 'Best hide all your ill-gotten gains, then.' The two men shared a throaty laugh as Giddings swung the door open and waved his visitors through. 'Third door on the right,' he barked. 'That's the records office.'

It was a dark and unwelcoming room with a single table at its centre. Piles of boxes blocked the light from the windows. Shelves lined every wall, some of them home to the greatest profusion of cobwebs that Bowman had seen for some time.

'Is there a system to all this?' Sergeant Graves gasped as he looked around. 'Some method of storage and retrieval?' He was suddenly afraid that he would be spending several hours in this airless room.

By way of a response, Giddings slammed a large book onto the table, sending clouds of dust into the air around them. Bowman resisted the urge to cough.

'Copenhagen Tunnel,' Giddings announced, pointedly. 'What do you need to know?'

'What is it?' Graves asked, simply.

Giddings sighed again. Sweeping his hat from his head, he rubbed his eyes in exasperation. When he spoke, it was with the impatient tones of a teacher to a pair of slow-witted children.

'What we know of as the Copenhagen Tunnel is actually three. The first was built under Copenhagen Fields some forty years ago, a mile out of King's Cross.'

'Hence the name,' Graves nodded.

Giddings blinked at the interruption. 'The second was built in Eighteen Eighty Seven and the third six years ago.'

Bowman turned to his companion. 'Harris has been at The Silver Cross for quite some time,' he mused.

Graves nodded. 'Certainly longer than the six years since

construction of the third tunnel, by all accounts.'

Bowman frowned. 'How old would you say he was?'

'Difficult to say,' Graves shrugged. Harris, with his leathery tanned skin and long hair, seemed as old as the hills. The more impolite of his customers would joke that he had served behind the bar for as long as there had been a drinking establishment on the site. The young sergeant knew that to be at least a couple of hundred years.

'It's certainly easy to believe he's in his sixties,' he concluded. 'Best look at the construction of the first tunnel, I'd say.'

Bowman nodded in agreement, then turned to the stout man beside him. Giddings had clearly been following their conversation. Before Bowman had opened his mouth to speak, he had already leafed through the volume before him and found the relevant entries.

'Thirteenth June, Eighteen Fifty,' he announced, swivelling the book round to face the inspector. 'Construction begins on the Copenhagen Tunnel.' He stabbed at the relevant entry with a chubby and tobacco-stained finger.

Bowman peered closer. Flicking through the pages with his thumb, he saw page after page of closely-written text in several colours of ink and in several different hands. The pages on the right were divided into columns and denoted dates and times of pertinent events, the moving of equipment and supply of provisions. It also included occasional entries of names connected with specific incidents. 'Dinklage, William,' read one. 'Dismissed, drunkard.' 'Roberts, Albert,' read another, 'injured.'

The pages on the left detailed the teams of men assigned to any given stretch of track. They were arranged in groups of four. No doubt, thought Bowman, one of them would have been in the position of supervisor.

'Where do we start?' breathed Sergeant Graves at the inspector's side.

'We look for any entry for Emmett Harris.'

'Should be easy enough,' puffed Giddings. 'The first tunnel was a relatively straightforward affair with only some four hundred teams.'

'But that's sixteen hundred names,' Bowman sighed. 'We may well have to take this book away with us, Mr Giddings.'

'No need, sir,' interjected Graves, suddenly. He was leaning forward over the table in his excitement. 'Look there.'

Bowman followed his gaze to an entry on a left hand page. Beneath a date, the Eighteenth of August, Eighteen Fifty, he could read the name *Emmett Harris*.

'And look.' Graves was sliding his finger down the page. 'Nathaniel Spendlove.' He moved his finger down again.

'Norman Atkinson,' Bowman read aloud.

'That would be the team,' offered Giddings, unbidden. 'The name above them would be the foreman.'

Bowman directed his gaze to the top of the list. 'Jacob Holly,' he read.

'Holly?' Giddings seemed suddenly taken aback.

Bowman straightened himself at the table. 'Is that pertinent, Mr Giddings?'

Giddings rubbed his great jaw as he thought for a while then, with a sudden flurry of activity, spun the book round to face him. Licking his fingers, he leafed frantically through its pages. 'Eighteen Fifty Two,' he said at last. 'The last stages of construction.' Again, he spun the book round so that the inspectors might read more easily.

There, on the left hand side, the same team was listed among many others. Holly, Atkinson, Harris and Spendlove. Tracing across to the opposite page with a finger, Bowman noticed an entry for the Twenty Third of February. 'Incident,' it read, simply. 'Atkinson, dismissed. Harris, dismissed. Spendlove, dismissed.' Bowman took a breath as he read the last entry. 'Holly, *deceased.*' He looked to Graves.

'What happened, Mr Giddings?' the sergeant asked, fearfully.

Giddings seemed suddenly engaged. 'Quite a famous case, actually,' he boomed, 'at least, that is, in railway circles.' He leaned his weight against the table. 'His was the only death recorded in the construction of that first tunnel, so the story has endured.'

Bowman could quite imagine. The life of a navvy was a dangerous one. To have only one such death on a stretch of track was an achievement, indeed.

'What is the incident referred to?'

Giddings was back at the shelves, retrieving another book from amongst the cobwebs. 'Jacob Holly was a hard man by all accounts, and would drive his men hard, too. He would cut corners to get ahead of schedule, then pocket the bonus himself. His men were tired and overworked but he cared not. Then, just as they were completing one of the last sections of the tunnel, several of the other teams pulled back for the day. But not Holly's. He worked his men into the night, determined to be the man to break through.' Giddings rolled a cigarette between his fingers as he spoke. The glint in his eye showed just how much he was enjoying himself. He seemed a different man entirely to the surly individual the detectives had met on the concourse. 'His team set explosives and retired to a distance to wait, but the explosives failed. Furious, Holly went to investigate.'

Graves winced. He had a feeling he knew what was coming next. Giddings nodded as if to confirm his suspicions. 'They found every part of him but his right arm.'

'Mr Giddings,' Bowman frowned, 'all this happened forty

years ago. How are you so conversant with the details?'

Giddings leaned forward to stab at the page. There, on the left hand side, the name 'Edward Giddings' was listed in another group of four.

'You were there?' Graves' eyes were wide.

Edward Giddings puffed out his chest. 'Been a railwayman all my life,' he said, proudly. 'First building 'em and now running 'em.'

Inspector Bowman felt a sudden respect for the man. 'You worked on the Copenhagen Tunnel?'

Giddings nodded, suddenly wistful. 'We heard the blast from where we were camped,' he whispered. 'We knew at once something was wrong.'

Bowman blinked. 'How so?'

'The blast was too big,' Giddings replied, simply. 'Turns out they had laid three times the explosives they needed.'

Graves sucked air in through his teeth.

'There were suspicions, of course,' concluded Giddings. 'But nothing was proven.'

Bowman narrowed his eyes. 'What do you think, Giddings?'

Giddings thought for a moment. 'His men were tired. He'd pushed them hard. Mistakes happen.'

Graves offered his thoughts. 'But it may not have been an accident?'

Giddings struck his match against a shelf and jammed his cigarette between his lips. 'Not for me to judge,' he said from the side of his mouth.

Bowman thought fast. Was the man who had served him faithfully at The Silver Cross only that very morning really responsible for Jacob Holly's death?

'Was there an inquiry?'

Giddings blew smoke into the already gloomy room. 'Naturally,' he said. 'And the findings are detailed here.' He opened the second book upon the table and leafed through its pages until he found his place. Bowman turned the book towards him.

'It says no further action would be taken beyond the men's dismissal.'

'Nothing could be proven either way, as I remember,' added Giddings.

'There is a petition here on behalf of his widow,' the inspector continued. 'She asked for a pension on account of his long service. It appears she had a son by him.' Bowman looked to Graves, pointedly. 'Her petition was refused.'

'He was only a baby, if memory serves,' said Giddings. The tip of his cigarette glowed a fierce red as he drew upon it.

Graves was thinking. 'So, he would be, what, in his forties now?'

'If he lived,' offered Giddings, cruelly.

'The holly found in Spendlove's hand,' said Bowman, turning to his young companion. 'Might that be meant as a symbol?'

Graves nodded. 'Perhaps something to do with Jacob Holly?'

'Or his son,' Bowman added.

Graves fell upon the first book again, flicking furiously through its pages in search of the list of names.

'Spendlove, we know about,' he said as he read it again. 'And Harris, of course. But we need to find this Norman Atkinson.'

'Ah,' interjected Giddings. 'Now there I might be of further assistance.'

The two detectives turned as one to face the man in the smart uniform.

'Go on,' Bowman entreated.

'We railwaymen stick together. Some years ago, I was approached by Atkinson.'

Bowman raised his eyebrows by way of encouragement.

'He was moving to London and was in search of rooms.'

Giddings spat a stray strand of tobacco from his tongue. 'I put him in touch with a landlord I knew.'

'Why was he moving to London?' Graves was enthralled. Giddings was proving to be more forthcoming than he could ever have imagined.

'To take up a position as rector at St Martin-In-The-Fields.'

'In Trafalgar Square?' asked Bowman, his moustache twitching. He remembered Spendlove's visit shortly after his argument with Harris.

'The very same,' Giddings confirmed. 'And for all I know, he is there to this day.'

'Sergeant Graves,' said Bowman, a note of urgency in his voice, 'get to Atkinson as soon as you can. Tell him he may be in danger. I'll go to Harris.'

Graves nodded as he turned to the door.

'Thank you for your time, Mr Giddings,' panted Bowman as he followed.

'Not at all,' replied Giddings without a trace of irony. 'It was a pleasure to be of assistance.'

It was dark already. The clock had barely struck three of the clock but, already, the sun had dropped below the rooftops. Graves knocked the snow from his shoes as he stood before St Martin-In-The-Fields. It had once stood shoulder to shoulder with other buildings until Trafalgar Square had been created. Now, it stood like a beacon on its east side, enjoying an open aspect that allowed the passing crowds to stop and gaze at its portico, pediment and supporting Corinthian columns.

Graves walked carefully up the wide steps and pushed at the door to gain entry. The church was empty. With the Christmas season over, mused Graves, most had had their fill of religiosity. With the door closed against the busy street, the interior of the church rang with a silence that almost hurt his ears. An arcade of columns stretched before him as he made his way slowly up the aisle. Candles flickered and guttered around him.

'Hello?' he called, only to hear his own voice echoing back from the vaulted ceiling. His eyes wandered across the galleries and vestibules that lined the building. Despite the gravity of the situation, he couldn't help but stare in admiration at the stucco cherubs, clouds and shells that adorned the panels around him.

Reaching the end of the aisle, Graves stopped before the altar. The ephemera of Christmas was still littered about the place. Candles and silverware stood amongst a selection of carved wooden figures arranged to represent a nativity scene. The sergeant lifted his gaze and stared in awe at the figure that hung on the cross above him. The silence pressed down upon him. He felt like an intruder upon some sacred event.

Just as he was about to turn and leave, he caught sight of an open door leading to the sacristy.

'Hello?' he called again. Nothing. Steeling himself, Graves walked across the cold flagstones and leaned against the door to open it further still. As his eyes adjusted to the gloom, he saw a shape on the floor. He took a breath as it resolved itself into the shape of a body. A man lay sprawled on the floor, his legs twisted beneath him. Just as Graves feared, a slick of blood oozed from a wound at his neck.

'Atkinson,' Graves whispered, kneeling beside him on the cold floor. As he leaned over the body, he noticed something clenched in Atkinson's fist. Unpeeling his fingers, he saw that he was clutching at a sprig of holly.

Inspector Bowman had left Graves at Charing Cross and turned down Whitehall towards The Silver Cross. Approaching through the crowds, he was surprised to see the tavern closed to customers, its doors locked and its shutters thrown across its windows. As he stood beneath the sign of the cross that hung from the storey above him, he heard a noise from the side of the building.

Fearing the worst, Bowman turned up his collar and picked his way carefully up the alley beside the tavern. The ice was harder here and, once or twice, Bowman had to reach out to the wall to keep from slipping. At last, he reached the end of the alley, where he saw the hatch to the tavern's cellar laying open in the path. Bowman could hear the scrape of wooden barrels being moved beneath his feet. As he bent to peer closer into the darkness, he was surprised by the appearance of a tousled head in the hole in the ground. He recognised Harris' lad at once. Bowman had often seen him scurrying about the bar, fetching and carrying. He guessed the boy was readying himself for the evening's trade, but where was Harris?

'Brompton cemetery,' said the boy, unbidden.

'I beg your pardon?' Bowman was taken aback.

'Drunk as a lord, he was.' The boy wiped his nose on a sleeve. 'Reckon something must've been botherin' him.'

'Harris?' Bowman squatted on his haunches. He needed to be certain they were talking about the same man.

'Of course, Harris. Who else would you be lookin' for? I arrived early for me day's work, only to find him nursin' a bottle of brandy.' The lad winked. 'I say nursin', attackin' more like.' He gave a cackle. 'I've never seen him so in his cups.' The urchin pulled his elbows up through the hatch and rested them on the dirty ground around him. 'He drained the bottle, mumbled somethin' about Brompton Cemetery, then bid me shut up shop.'

'Do you know why?'

'No idea.' The boy sighed. 'I only hope he gets back in time for the evening rush. I won't get paid otherwise.'

Bowman nodded in sympathy. 'And you're sure he said

Brompton Cemetery?'

'Aw, not you as well,' the boy moaned. 'I know what he said.
I ain't deaf.'

Bowman gave a half-smile as he rose. Stretching his legs to
restore some feeling, he leaned against the wall to start his
return journey back down the alley. A sudden thought struck
him.

'What do you mean, *not you as well*?' He turned to face the
boy in the hatch.

'Can't a boy be left to get on with his work?' the lad
complained. He rolled his eyes. 'You're the second man to ask
after Harris in the past half hour. I've never known him be so
popular.' He gave a smirk.

'Someone else has asked for him?'

'Bloke with a missing eye,' the boy confirmed. 'He was most
persistent, too.'

The snow fell as a blanket upon the city, lending an air of
peaceful serenity to the graves and monuments that stood in
Brompton Cemetery. Once a pastoral landscape just three miles
from the centre of London, the cemetery lay between Old
Brompton and Fulham Roads, on the western border of the
Royal Borough of Kensington and Chelsea. Built in response to
the growing population and the lack of space in which to bury
its dead, it was one of seven park cemeteries created around the
capital. And it had filled up quickly.

For the richest in society, here was an opportunity to be laid
to rest in conspicuous grandeur. Granite and marble
mausoleums lined the central avenue. They loomed through the
bare lime trees, the final place of repose for generations of the
same family. Stone angels stood as perpetual mourners over
other plots in a great circle bordered with impressive
colonnades. Wide steps led down to iron doors, beyond which

lay the catacombs. Here, the less prosperous could be laid on shelves to await their eternity in God's judgement.

Emmett Harris wove his way through the plainer headstones beyond the circle towards a collection of graves beneath a high wall. He mumbled wildly to himself, his eyes peering through his curtain of hair as he trudged through the virgin snow. He held a bottle in his hands and paused only to take the occasional slug, wincing as it hit the back of his throat.

'Forgive us!' he called as he neared the graves. 'Forgive us all!'

He stopped at the granite wall that soared above him and reached out to a plaque that had been fixed there. 'Dedicated to the memory of those who fell in the construction of the railways,' it read, 'this plot provided in lasting gratitude by the Amalgamated Society of Railway Engineers.' Harris ran his trembling fingers over the symbol of two crossed hammers and a stretch of railway leading from a tunnel. A string of drool hung from his lips. 'Forgive us,' he whispered.

'You are the last,' rasped a voice from behind him.

Harris spun round, clutching at his head in his drunken delirium. He focussed his eyes on a man beneath a nearby yew tree. Harris was alarmed to see he had only one eye.

'Emmett Harris, you are the last.'

'I am sorry,' wailed Harris as he fell to his knees, heedless of the snow. 'Spare me!'

The man's voice was thick with anger. 'As you spared my father?' He reached into his pocket. Harris sobbed as he saw the man retrieve a knife, the cold metal of its blade flashing in the white light.

'Before you die,' the man continued, 'you will know my story. I am the son of Jacob Holly.'

Harris nodded weakly. 'We learned of you at the inquiry,' he whispered. 'You must believe it was an accident.' He wrapped his arms around himself in search of solace, his great sobs shaking his body.

Holly gazed dispassionately at the wretch before him. 'It matters not,' he said simply. 'A life for a life.'

'But three? If I am the last, then you have already taken Atkinson as well as Spendlove. If a life for a life, then why take three?'

Holly was trembling as he fought to maintain control of his ire. 'One each for the lives you took,' he hissed. 'Spendlove was for my father, Atkinson was for my mother. But you...' he held his knife before him. '*You are for me.*'

Harris looked about him as if help might be found in the graves and mausoleums. He rose slowly to his feet, his legs barely able to support him.

Holly held him in his gaze. 'My mother and I were left to the mercy of the workhouse when the railways refused to give her a pension.' He fixed his remaining eye on the plaque on the wall and spat. 'All we got for my father's life was a communal grave.' He turned to scan the stones before him. Each, he knew, marked the spot where several workers lay. All had lost their lives on the railways, but none had been deemed worthy of name on a stone. The only marking was the insignia of the Amalgamated Society.

'We were young,' Harris was pleading as he scanned his surroundings for a way out. His head was pounding and he was struggling to think clearly. 'Your father worked us hard. We were tired and not thinking straight.'

'Not one of you thought to check the explosives?' Holly boomed. 'Not one of you thought to question it?'

Harris shook his head, aware that any explanation would be insufficient for the vengeful spirit before him. 'We were young,' he repeated, feebly.

'You have lived a life,' Holly suddenly wailed. 'A life that was denied to my father and mother.'

Harris' lip quivered. He peered through the snow towards the grand entrance to the cemetery. He was sure he could make out a dark shape resolving itself in the sleet.

'After she died, I joined the army to find purpose,' Holly continued, 'but I was abandoned once more at Majuba. Left for dead by those I trusted, just like my father before me.' He took a step nearer his quarry. Fumbling in the folds of his coat, he took a sprig of holly from a pocket. 'I left this as a marker on the other two, to show my father his death had been avenged.' He stretched out a hand and held the holly before him. 'Take it,' he hissed.

Harris reached out, knowing all the while that a cold death awaited him. Soon, he knew, he would be lying in the snow, his hot blood melting the ice.

'A last drink?' he implored, his words slurred.

Holly nodded as the landlord raised his bottle to his lips. Grateful, Harris closed his eyes and prepared to take his last drink upon this Earth. The last thing he expected was for the bottle to be blasted from his hands. A loud crack rent the air about him, echoing off the stone wall at his back.

Cautiously, Harris opened his eyes, first one and then the other. Holly stood before him, his knife held weakly in his fist. He had dropped the sprig of holly to the ground and now stood, mesmerised by a hole that had appeared below his shoulder. He reached up to grab at his clothing where a slick of blood had started to soak through from his skin. He blinked furiously, searching Harris' eyes for an explanation. As Holly pitched forward, Harris saw the figure of Detective Inspector Bowman standing immediately behind him, his revolver raised. He had a look of intense concentration on his face as he drew a whistle from his pocket and blew hard.

'I thought I was a dead man,' Harris whispered, his voice

cracking with relief.

'Not today, Harris,' replied Bowman as he lurched forwards to restrain the man in the snow. 'Not today.'

He heaved Holly to his feet. Holding his hands behind him, Bowman marched him unceremoniously back towards the cemetery entrance, there to enlist the help of the local constables who were, even now, running towards him.

Harris was left to collect his thoughts and follow him unsteadily, but not before his gaze had fallen upon the sprig of holly in the snow. It had settled where his dreadful assailant had dropped it, its leaf as sharp as any needle, its berry as red as any blood.

Following the events in Brompton Cemetery, Harris had presented himself, sober, at Scotland Yard to give the inspector the whole of his story. Bowman had listened intently before deciding that the landlord had nothing to answer for. As far as he was concerned, the findings of the original inquiry stood. Even so, four days passed before Bowman dared to set foot in The Silver Cross.

At last, Sergeant Graves convinced him to enjoy a drink to mark the passing of the old year. The two men sat in their usual places, their damp coats steaming on a hook by the chimney breast. Bowman knocked the moisture from the brim of his hat and placed it on the table as he sat in his favourite chair by the fire. The tavern was particularly lively tonight, marked the inspector, and the two detectives sat in the glow of the fire as, it seemed, the whole of London descended upon The Silver Cross.

Having noticed their arrival from behind the bar, Emmett Harris poured two pints of porter and steeled himself. Marching to the table by the fire, he passed each man their drink and leaned in close.

'No, Harris, I will not permit it,' said Bowman before the

landlord could even open his mouth. 'We have had too many drinks upon the house.' He reached into his pockets and pulled out a wallet. 'In fact,' he continued, 'I will pay for my drink and Graves' drink.' He raised his voice to be heard above the melee in the saloon. 'And a drink for every man and woman in this bar, in a mark of respect and admiration for its landlord, Emmett Harris.'

A great cheer rose from the assembled drinkers and a few of them embarked upon a chorus or two of 'For He's A Jolly Good Fellow', before rushing at the bar with their empty tankards. Harris was only too happy to oblige them, pulling at the taps as if a man possessed, his lank hair falling into his face as he smiled back at the detectives by the fireplace.

'So, you saw Holly at Spring Gardens?' Graves took a draft from his glass. He had barely seen Bowman these last few days. The sergeant had been busy with paperwork and was eager to hear the final details of the case.

Bowman nodded. 'When I saw Harris' altercation with Spendlove. Little did I know I was conversing with the man who would kill them both.'

'Then Spendlove led Holly to Harris?' Graves shook his head.

'And then to Atkinson at St Martin-In-The-Fields. Harris says Spendlove found the sprig of holly on his bar at The Salisbury Stores and was concerned at its significance.'

Graves' blue eyes were wide. 'Concerned enough to warn the others,' he said with a sudden understanding.

'Holly was just lucky that the three men had settled in such close proximity to each other.'

'As Giddings said at King's Cross, railwaymen stick together.'

Bowman lifted his glass to his lips. 'Particularly those who have been through so much together.'

The young sergeant looked towards the bar where Harris was

busying himself cleaning glasses. He felt pity for the landlord, that he should be so haunted by an event from forty years ago. 'I suppose we're all prisoners to our past,' he murmured.

'Not all of us, Graves,' Bowman smiled, holding his companion's gaze. 'Some of us have escaped it, with help from our friends.' The two men clinked their glasses and sipped from their drinks as the bell rang.

'That's it, sir,' beamed Graves, wiping the froth from his upper lip. 'Midnight.'

A cheer rang out in the saloon bar.

Bowman looked into the fire. 'So it is.'

'Which means,' continued Graves, leaning across the table, 'that I am now a detective inspector.'

It took a moment for the news to sink in. Bowman's moustache twitched as he turned back. Graves was nodding. 'I had the news over Christmas, but I couldn't seem to find the right time to tell you. Effective from the first day of January.'

Bowman sprung from his seat to clap the new inspector on the shoulder. 'Why, Anthony, that is marvellous news, indeed!' A rueful look settled upon his face. 'I shall miss you.'

Graves laughed. 'You won't be getting rid of me that easily,' he grinned. 'I dare say you'd be welcome in my office from time to time.' His eyes sparkled with a mischief that Bowman had come to adore. 'By appointment, of course.'

The two men laughed as Bowman sank back into his chair.

'Thank you, sir,' said Graves. 'I know you smoothed the way for me.'

Bowman shook his head, indignant at the very suggestion. 'I did no such thing, Graves. I merely suggested to the commissioner that you were just the sort of man who would excel as an inspector. And just the sort of man we need in such a post. You're an asset to the Yard.' He raised his glass.

'I'll drink to that,' said Graves, raising his own.

Bowman took a breath and looked at the young man before him. It had been quite a year, and not one he'd care to live through again. He met Graves' eyes and smiled.

'Happy New Year, Detective Inspector Graves,' he said.

Printed in Great Britain
by Amazon

73687891R00118